Poison Princess

Sylvia Morrow

Dedication

To
Love
Justice
Second Chances
And Revenge.

Content Notes

Prison, murder, explicit sex, deadly poison, loss of virginity, fictional government and military, trouble finding a job, poverty, bigotry, implied sex work, bullying, unethical human experimentation, abusive foster family history, police brutality, main character arrested, parent death, food tampering, solitary confinement, mental torture, talk of weight change, car death mention, mention of bugs, boats, the ocean, groped by stranger in public, illness, wounds, mention of children harmed in Supervillain attack, needles, eye injury, MMC has sex with someone else (one night stand, not detailed) before he gets with the FMC, tail play, depression.

Any further questions, concerns, or suggestions should be sent to the author at sylviamorrowauthor@gmail.com

Places to Know

Capital City

The biggest city in the country. First city to make superheroes and Supervillains known to the public. Where the Supervillain attack known as The Big Mash-Up occurred.

Waljean's on Prospect Place

Part of a chain of pharmacies. One of the few places in the Capital City area willing to hire former Villains. Where Tabitha and Henry work.

Gnistra Lake Penitentiary

Federal Maximum Security Prison outside of Capital City. Reconfigured to hold Supervillains.

Geiger Falls Research Institute

Government research facility where top-secret, unethical human experiments are conducted. Situated on a rocky island off the coast of Capital City.

Fort Jeffries

The military base closest to Capital City.

Capital County Jail

The jail where all Villains and Heroes in the entirety of Capital City County are held after arrest.

New Day Tower

Government subsidized housing for formerly incarcerated Supervillains.

Sandra's Diner

Mashie-friendly diner. Originally owned by the same Sandra of Sandra's cafe but sold in the early years after the Mash-Up. Open late.

On Our Last Episode

THE GOOD CITIZENS OF Capital City were blissfully unaware of the existence of an entirely different class of humans. These othered city dwellers were gifted—sometimes at birth, sometimes through the power of science—with extraordinary abilities. Though a worldwide phenomenon, most of them lived in and around Capital City. The few who did know of these secret citizens referred to them as "the Blessed" or "Deviants," depending on how they viewed them. Those in charge only called them *necessary*. Like a moth to flame, the government sought out these powered people for their own cryptic purposes, forcing them to stay hidden from the public and living in the shadows...

Until Darkiss changed everything ten years ago.

Flying over the city, stopping high above Capital Square, Darkiss flooded the airwaves to let the world know that he, and others like him, existed.

The citizens were inferior to the Blessed, he proclaimed, stupid, cruel, ruining the planet. Too many. Without a shred of remorse, he informed them that he was eliminating half of them.

In an instant, Darkiss combined each citizen of Capital City with one other person. It killed neither of them but instead put both people's minds into one body. The reporters later called this "mashing."

As people disappeared from their vehicles, their work, and abandoned their children in an instant—chaos took over.

In the end, people *did* die.

A small minority of victims were 'mashed' with animals. The most common were dogs and cats, but some were stuck with other creatures (though always mammals). Though labeled "Mashies" as a slur initially, the term was used so commonly that it became official.

Several gifted individuals tried and failed to apprehend Darkiss. Just when it seemed like he would get away with his crimes, a Hero named Honor Man flew in to save the day, engaging in an epic battle high above Capital Park until that dastardly Villain was finally vanquished. Honor Man became a Hero, symbolizing justice not only to Capital City, but to the entire world.

The public had no clue what happened to Darkiss after that, only that he was defeated, gone, his henchmen taken to prison. The newly created Bureau for the Management and Study of Aberrant Genetics promised the citizens they were safe. For most, that was good enough.

The entire event was called "The Big Mash-Up" by a popular newscaster. It stuck, though most people disliked the name. Attempts at calling it something more fittingly serious have failed.

After a few years, all but the unfortunate Mashies were returned to their original bodies. Most of the city was rebuilt. *The Blessed* became part of every-day life.

Those working for the good of the citizens are referred to as Superheroes, or Heroes. The criminals are referred to as Supervillains or Villains. Being unclassified, in between, or neutral is not allowed when you're gifted.

Not in Capital City.

In our next episode, ten years after The Big Mash-Up, we find one of Darkiss's closest confidants recently released from prison.

Can she be trusted to live peacefully among the good citizens of Capital City? Or will she always poison everything she touches?

Capital City Review

Volume 10, Issue 3 March 2015

POISON PRINCESS CAUGHT

NOTORIOUS MURDERESS TABITHA LIMA ARRESTED

The People Celebrate

Mugshot Taken at Capital County Jail

Tabitha Lima, better known to the people of Capital City as Poison Princess, was arrested last night. The successful capture was a team effort that took Capital City police force's own Villain Response Team as well as the Bureau for the Management and Study of Aberrant Genetics' task force, to bring the killer in. Several lives were lost during the arrest, though police have not released their names at this time out of respect for the families.

Other unnamed Villains and criminals were found and arrested in the same location. Of the infamous four Villains who arrived with Darkiss the day of the Big Mash-Up, only Bradley "Stonecrash" Jones remains

at large. Klaire "Klaire Voyant" Feinberg, and Angela "Angelust" Smith were taken in earlier this week.

Little is known about the origins of Poison Princess, and her hideout gave no further hints. Lima was found in the luxury penthouse of former real estate mogul-turned small-time Villain, Golden Mirror. It's no surprise that one of

Darkiss's minions would choose to hide in a place of comfort and wealth; the jaw-droppingly lavish lair where the five stayed before they were forced to flee has been well-reported on. There will be no luxurious place to sleep for Tabitha now, however, and hopefully never again.

Lima's first court appearance is set for Monday, and is closed to the public.

Chapter One

Tabitha

How do I say "hello" in an employable way? More importantly, a way that would make a hiring manager forget about a bunch of murders? Despite trying for days, I don't think I have it down yet, and I'm running out of time.

Another deep breath. I clear my throat, and then, "Hi, I'm Tabitha."

Eh. I don't know. I think I'm going to sound like a depressed cheese grater no matter how long I practice. With a sigh of disgusting self-pity, I flop onto my futon. I tug on my boots, pick up the remote, and sink back into the pillows. May as well sit here and watch TV for a couple of minutes to waste time before the bus comes.

A familiar woman jumpscares me on the screen. Her green hair, tan skin splashed with bright colors and crossed with dark stripes, eyes black and soulless as an insect, are a daily sight. *Oh, joy*. It's my own weird face. *Bleh*.

Jenna O'Leary, the reporter from the Capital City Tribune, managed to get our interview to air at prime-time last night. Apparently, it was popular enough that they're still replaying clips this morning.

Even though I hate watching myself, I pause to do so this time. With what I've got planned for today, it couldn't hurt to practice my interview skills.

"So, Ms. Lima," the reporter on the TV asks. "He could have included you and the other three in The Big Mash-Up—yet he chose not to. How does that make you feel?"

Is that really how I look? *Oh, no.* No wonder the reporter looks like she's halfway to running out of there. I have all the charm of a tick on a dick.

"I'm not fond of him, if that's what you're asking," I reply. "We weren't friends. The only reason he didn't transform us like he did everyone else in the city was that he needed his little army."

Well, there's a *tiny* bit of light in my face at the end when I mention my former cohorts. *Klaire Voyant, Angelust, Stonecrash.* Add me—*Poison Princess*—and we made the most badass group of teens there ever was. Well, until we got arrested. That part sucked.

"I see," Jenna says. "Can you tell us why you were chosen to be one of his comrades?"

I watch as she leans in as if she's going to get a really juicy answer. She gets absolutely *nada* in return.

"I can't legally discuss that as part of the Villain rehabilitation program," I reply.

There's not much more after that because the Villain rehabilitation program really does prevent me from answering a lot of questions people want answers to. If I could tell the whole world about how they kidnapped me, tortured me, mixed me up with frog DNA, and gave me poison skin, I'd gladly do it. But, sorry, Ms. O'Leary, I'm not going back to prison.

I'm getting a retail job.

Chapter Two

Henry

"Help! Call the police! We need Honor Man!"

The plastic spoon clacks against the table as my nephew calls for the city's strongest superhero to save him from... my cooking. I lean back on the sofa, cross my arms, and wait for a moment of calm. There are many more clickety-clacks before that moment comes. Finally, he looks me over thoughtfully and sets down his spoon to nervously wring his pudgy little hands.

"Henny?" he asks, his blue eyes growing bigger than they already are.

"Hen-ry," I correct him.

He sighs in a way that's far too adult for a two-and-a-half-year-old and picks the spoon up again. I cover my mouth to hide my grin as he waves it around in frustration.

"Listen here, Henny," he says, an exact imitation of his father. This kid is too cute and too smart. He points at me with the spoon. "How come you got a tail?"

As my long, rat-like, prehensile tail slithers out from between the cushions to make an appearance, I raise an eyebrow at him. This is a stalling tactic so that he doesn't have to eat his carrots, I'm certain of it.

"Jimmy, you know why. Remember?"

He nods, chestnut brown curls flopping over his forehead. "You got mashed. With a... *napossum*."

An opossum, but close enough.

"Yep. You got it."

He wiggles in his seat with his eyes locked on my tail. I can see the gears turning in his head, and I prepare myself for another question. So far, that's as much as he's asked about my unfortunate situation.

"But how did you get mashed?"

Now, it's my turn to sigh. Every parent in Capital City has to have this discussion with their kid someday, but I'll leave the fine details to my bro.

"A big, bad Villain got me," I start, but quickly reach forward when Jimmy clutches his spoon nervously. I smile, stroke his hair, and plant a smooch on his forehead. "But don't worry, he's all gone now."

His little body *mostly* relaxes, but his eyes still look worried. He looks at me and asks, "Are there more Villains?"

I pull him out of his chair, tug him into my lap, and squeeze him tight. I *really* do not want to step on parenting toes here, but I also don't want to leave him sitting there worried about bad guys until Mark picks him up.

"I'll let your dad tell you more about it, okay? There's a lot to talk about. Just know that *even if* a Villain were here, no one would hurt you."

"Cuz you would save me, huh? Right, Henny?" He says with all the confidence in the world.

As he flops his now-soothed and smiling head onto my shoulder, my tail decides on its own to wrap around his arms, then tickle his cheek. He giggles and buries his head in my armpit.

It's hard not to think of all the kids I was sup-posed to protect on the day of The Big Mash-Up. Half of them disappeared right in front of me. There was *nothing* I could do about it, and no way I could have prevented it.

Yet, I stroke Jimmy's hair anyway, and I smile. I do it because I love him, and because he doesn't know any better. Not yet.

"Yep, me and your dad will protect you, buddy." He reaches up to tug on the one white streak in my floppy, ginger hair—a stray bit of the opossum in my DNA, and a particular fascination of his—but I catch his hand and pretend to nibble on it. When he's done squealing with laughter, I look him in the eyes, serious as a funeral, and remind him, "But no one is going to protect you from those carrots."

Chapter Three

Tabitha

THE MONEY FROM THAT stupid interview covers rent for this month. There's no way I would have done TV if I didn't need the cash, but I refuse to live in the government-subsidized housing offered to former Villains. Those places are disgusting.

"Hello, sweetie," old Ms. Lee, who lives in the apartment across from me, says as I enter the lobby. "How are you today?"

"Fine," I reply, same as always.

I hang back in a dusty corner, giving her plenty of space. And yet, she still goes out of her way to pat me on the shoulder as she goes by. I cringe, even though I know she should be safe. I'm wearing all my layers.

"That's nice to hear. Good to know you kids are behaving." She smiles, her cloudy eyes looking a little brighter behind her thick glasses. "Have a lovely day."

After she's gone, I brush the dust and cobwebs off my clothes—*okay, the lobby might need some dusting, but at least it's not decaying and full of cockroaches like the Villain housing*—and head to the bus.

Hopefully, today's the day I get lucky with employment. Since being discharged from Gnistra Lake Penitentiary, I've managed to scrounge up money here and there, but just barely. I've been a hustler by necessity since before I could read, but that doesn't mean I haven't stopped trying to find a *regular* job. It would be nice to have a regular paycheck for once in my life. Just to see how it feels, if nothing else.

Before they decided to let us *bad guys* out of prison, Congress made a law that employers can't discriminate against rehabilitated Villains in the hiring process. They still do, though. All the time. They're just not obvious about it to outsiders.

That caused a big problem for the politicians. Too many of us ended up homeless due to a lack of funds. The *good* voters didn't like seeing the criminal freak show hanging around their neighborhood, begging for change. The government liked it even less when they didn't know where said freaks were.

So, the good old Bureau for the Management and Study of Aberrant Genetics stepped in. They needed to keep track of us, and what better solution than to put all the little piggies in one pen? They provided the housing for free—a single rundown, disgusting apartment building called New Day Tower—to get a ratings boost from the citizens... and to make sure Villains had no excuse not to comply.

Three floors does not a *tower* make, in my opinion, but I'm a nobody, apparently.

Anyway, it was just big enough to house all the formerly incarcerated Villains and a shitload of cockroaches. No thanks.

I'll make it on my own. Just need money.

Another former Villain living on his own told me there's a drugstore chain that hires our kind. The founder's son was a felon, and he strongly believes in second chances. A job in the stock room would mean no touching people and minimal talking.

I'm nervous, though. Interacting with people is difficult—not surprising when you consider I was in prison for the last ten years. Before that, I was on a murder spree, and before that, I was a science experiment. My job interview skills are understandably nonexistent.

I did buy a mirror, though. Been practicing how to smile naturally. The results are... grim. Need more practice.

The thick powder and anti-perspirant I wear each day to prevent sweating through my clothes is really getting a workout. I tuck my hair into my hood and take a deep breath. It's okay. I've been to other interviews. It's fine.

As the bus drives closer, I double-check that my conspicuous hair is tucked into my hood. I don't want people looking at me. I attract more attention than I want to already.

Whenever I leave the house, I cover myself from head to toe. I have to wear gloves, a hood, and boots—complete coverage. No exceptions, except for the front of my face (with a scarf I can pull up when necessary). No one will be poisoned by me again.

Besides, if I didn't cover up, then people would recognize me. It's not like every person you pass has the facial markings of a poison dart frog. And when people recognize me, well... they're rarely fans.

I pull the black hood as far forward as it can go before stepping onto the bus. No more time to worry. I need a job, and I plan to get one.

Capital City, prepare yourself—I'm on a mission.

When the bus driver announces the Prospect Place stop, I ring the bell. As I push through the crowded aisle to get to the exit, every touch to the fabric on my body makes me wince. A man in a dirty, red sweatshirt gropes my ass with one of his crusty hands. I bare my teeth under my hood but don't react—I can't. If I respond at all, I might lose my temper. Lose control. And if I lose control on him, then everyone on this bus will suffer, including me.

The bus drops me off safely in front of the store. Perfect. I tug my hood forward once more and make sure my gloves are pulled up all the way. *Deep breath. I'm a productive citizen. I'm trustworthy, and I won't kill anyone. You can count on it.*

Ding

Fluorescent lights and a twenty-year-old pop song greet me inside the drugstore. I attempt to appear confident as I stride to the nearest cashier, a gangly teenager. I can feel that my footsteps are too hard, and my arms are swinging too wide, but I can't do anything about it.

"I'm here to speak with your manager. About a job," I say from under my hood. It comes out sounding like a demand. I'm glad he can't see me wince.

"Oh, uh, one second," the teen replies, voice cracking, before calling for his manager over the intercom.

A moment later, a short, chubby lady with a big, bright smile comes out of a room off to the side of the registers to greet me.

"Well, hello there! You must be Tabitha. I'm Milly. Why don't you come on back and let's have a chat, yeah?" She sounds like the type of television mother who makes casserole.

The room she leads me to is cramped and dim. We each sit on an office chair on either side of a metal table. There's that sticker stuff on the top of the table that makes it look like fake wood, and I desperately want to peel it off. I somehow just know it would be satisfying. *No. Don't destroy the property. Look at something else.* There's a big box of store-brand paper towels on my left. Corkboards line the walls with all sorts of things tacked onto them. All said, I find this room much more pleasant than the wide-open brightness outside of it.

"So, you're here for the job in the backroom? Have you worked a job like that before?" she asks as she looks through my—very short—application.

"No, ma'am. I've never worked at any job before."

I swallow my shame. It's not my fault, I don't have any experience. I have to remember that. The government is the one that did this to me. Since I'm the one fixing it, I should be proud, not ashamed.

"It can be physically demanding. Are you able to lift up to fifty pounds? And stand for eight hours a day? Safely operate heavy machinery?"

"Yes, ma'am. If anything, I'm more capable than most physically. And I have the drive to work."

"That's very good. Now, I don't like asking this next part, but it's necessary." She sets down the papers and folds her hands on the table. "When the company hires rehabilitated Villains, we've found they each tend to have some kind of restriction—or, well, a reason they were unable to work a *normal* job before prison. We've decided it's easier to ask up front if you have any... *issues* that may be trouble down the road. Better to find out now than later."

Well, here it goes.

"I have to be covered at all times, including wearing gloves. If I don't, I could poison someone. It's not optional."

The woman frowns, propping her fist under her chin and staring at me, judging me. I shift uncomfortably in my seat. *I do not wish to be perceived.*

"But if you're covered, then you're fine? You're sure you won't hurt anyone?"

"Yes, ma'am. I definitely don't want to kill anyone again."

Milly sits a little farther back in her seat. I suppose that last sentence was unnecessary. *This is why I try to keep my responses to one or two words at a time. Ugh.*

"Can you work Sunday mornings?"

"Yes, ma'am."

"Promise you won't call in sick all the time?"

"Yes, ma'am," I say, attempting one of the smiles I practiced in the mirror. This one feels pretty good. Almost natural.

"Okey dokey, then." She slaps her hands flat on the table, pushing her chair backward. "Let's take you to the backroom and show you where you'll be working."

"I got the job? That's it?" Stunned, I don't move from my spot.

"Yep, but I'm a busy lady, so let's hurry up."

I got the job!

The smile worked!

"Yes, ma'am."

Chapter Four

Henry

"Ah! Shit ass dick motherfucker cunt—"

"Henry!" Milly snaps from the doorway.

Shaking out my slowly bruising hand, I try to turn my grimace into a smile.

"Sorry, Milly. Slammed my hand between two crates."

"A foul mouth won't make it any better. Do you need an incident report form?" she asks, clutching her clipboard to her chest.

"Nah, I'll be fine."

"Alright. I'm going to show your new coworker around, so be on your best behavior, please."

I salute Milly with my uninjured hand, then wave to the dark mass of person-shaped fabric next to her. The woman is wearing so many layers of clothing that she's basically black laundry with boots. But she's TALL. I'm not a short guy by any means, and from over here it looks like she just might be taller than I am.

Which is *hot*.

They start to walk my way, so I scramble to get back to stacking boxes. *Yep, just stacking boxes of toilet paper. Not ogling the new chick. Nope. Minding my own business, not obsessed with finding out who's under there.*

"And this is where we keep the back stock. You'll be working here. Henry will train you."

"Ooh, fun!" I cheerfully shake a 1000-ply roll, hoping she'll look up and show me her face.

No luck. The beautiful giantess denies me the pleasure of witnessing her glorious visage.

"I promise it's easy. You'll take to it right away. Do you have any questions so far?" Milly asks her.

"Yeah." The girl looks in my direction, but, unfortunately, I still can't make out her features. In a smoky, almost monotone voice, she says, "Is that a *rat* tail?"

I freeze. I thought I tucked that thing away. How embarrassing.

"I, uh, well—"

"Tabitha," Milly says carefully, "Here at Waljean's Pharmacy and Gifts, we don't ask each other about our Hero, Villain, or Mashie status. That includes questions about superpowers and animal parts. It's in the employee handbook, which we'll go over after the tour."

"Okay. Some people are sensitive, I guess." Tabitha shrugs. "What's this for?"

She points to the box crusher, and I let out a frustrated huff. I'm not *sensitive,* but explaining this stupid tail is annoying. I'm thankful I didn't get any really crazy animal features in the Mash-Up. I would have died if I ended up with a fucking marsupial pouch or pointy snout—but still. No one wants to be the guy with the opossum tail.

No one wants to be a *Mashie* at all.

Tabitha continues her tour of the back room, and I can't help watching her out of the corner of my eye. Sometimes out of the front of my eyes. She's so distracting. Just this big, hot, goth...

Ugh, step on me, please.

Son of a bitch, I haven't even seen her face yet, and she's got me by the dick. I really have to get myself under control. I mean, okay—maybe I've indulged in a few too many fetish videos. Maybe my social skills could use some work. But... I forgot my point.

"Henry, your tail," Milly whispers.

"Huh?" A box of tissues falls to the ground. I look behind me and realize it's knocking over more boxes. Yet again.

Tabitha is standing next to Milly with her gloved hand raised to her hooded face. I wonder what's up with the gloves. *Ooh,* maybe she's hiding an animal feature. That's gotta be it. I bet she's a Mashie too.

"Oh, my bad." I turn around to pick up the boxes, forgetting one very important detail. *The stupid tail.*

It smacks Tabitha right on her head. I snap around to apologize—and watch her hood slide off.

I gasp when I see what—*who*—is underneath. *It can't be.* But it is. Those are the solid black eyes, blue lips, patterned cheeks, and green hair I've seen hundreds of times before.

Poison Princess.

She scrambles to pull her hood back up, then heads toward the exit back into the main area of the store. Milly follows. I can't help but stand in shock, arms full of tissue boxes, jaw hanging open. *I was in the same room as Poison Princess.*

I have a poster of her at the end of my bed. She's the screensaver on my computer. This is... *wow.*

Poison Princess asked me about my tail.

This is the best day of my life.

Chapter Five

Tabitha

Back home. Alone, thank God. I can't believe I start the job tomorrow. That's so soon! I'm not sure I'm ready, but I'm going to *make* myself ready no matter what. I can't miss this opportunity.

I mess around in the kitchen for a while, cutting my chicken up just right so there aren't any weird parts in it. I like every bit to be exactly the same—easily identifiable morsels with no odd textures or colors. All the vegetables are perfectly chopped as well. No surprises.

Between the institute and the prison, I'm screwed up in the head when it comes to food. But I'm making this my way, so it'll be okay. It's a big batch that'll last me a while, too, which is important. Frugality is the *most* important part of my diet these days.

One thing I miss about my time with Darren? We had money. *Lots* of it.

Oh, and the fashion. We looked *good*. The whole army of Villains was stunning, especially his inner circle. Darren would not allow anyone to represent us poorly by walking about in shabby clothes, and honestly, none of us would have wanted to. Our Villain "costumes" were always way hotter than the ones the Heroes had. Functional too, of course.

The black hooded sweater I was wearing today is draped over the back of my ratty sofa. It's getting a bit faded and pilled already. I won't be able to replace it anytime soon, so it had better last.

I never used the hood I wore in the old days to hide from the world out of shame and fear, like I do this one. I wanted the world to see what the government did to me. I hardly wore anything then, aside from a spandex monokini, thigh-high boots, and my cape—all of them in black, trimmed with a poisonous shade of green.

A knock comes at my front door. I haven't been expecting anyone, and when you have as few friends as I do, a knock at the door is an unwelcome sound. I wash my hands quickly, then cautiously open the door.

"Hello, officer. How can I help you?" I ask, very carefully, when I see who's beyond it.

I'm no fan of the police, and they're certainly no fan of me. Because of my abilities, my history, and our known dislike of one another, I must be careful to remain polite and to always move slowly around them. There's far too high a chance that one will panic and shoot if I seem too aggressive.

"Ma'am, we've gotten reports that the building was defaced. I'm going to need you to come down to the station to speak with me about this and let me know what you were doing last night. If you could—"

"What?" I can't help but interrupt him. Me? Deface my own building? "That doesn't make sense. What do you mean by defacing?"

"If you could just come with me, we'll get this all settled."

"But I didn't do anything. Don't they have cameras or something?"

"You can ask questions downtown. Now, you either come with me willingly, or I call up a Villain response team and make it their problem. You decide."

If he calls a VRT, it could alert the Bureau, and they would have an excuse to send me back to prison. I *do not* want that. My shoulders slump.

"Fine. Let me turn off the stove."

When I turn to walk the short way back to my kitchen, I hear a familiar snap—the sound of a taser being removed from its holster. *Are you fucking shitting me?*

"I said to come with me," the officer barks.

"I have chicken in the frying pan. If I don't turn off the stove, this whole building will burn down. Do you want that?" I grind out between my teeth. *What is wrong with this imbecile?*

"You're not fooling me. Put your hands up!" he shouts, then pushes a button on the device on his shoulder and says, "I need backup. Uncooperative. Deviant with poison skin. Possible Villain response team required."

"You have got to be kidding. The stove is eight feet away. I can *smell* it cooking."

"Get on the ground!"

"Oh, fuck this." I stomp over to the stove and turn the dial off just before the hooks of the taser hit my back.

I know I did the right thing, making sure the building didn't burn down, but damn it feels bad right now. Future concerns don't seem very relevant when I'm writhing on my kitchen floor, electricity coursing through my body as a sweaty cop smelling like a dirty jockstrap screams in my face.

A bit of silver shines from under my oven. *Oh, a quarter. Nice.*

He tases me again, even though I'm not doing anything wrong. *Great, cool.* He approaches slowly as I writhe in pain. I shriek loudly, staring him dead in the eyes, and he hesitates. After a moment, he reconsiders approaching and takes a step back, keeping a steady watch until backup arrives.

More cops storm into my house, shouting because they don't know what to do with my bare skin.

I would have gladly put my gloves and hoodie on, officers, but now I can't move, sorry. Your problem now.

It takes them an hour to get someone in who can handle my toxic mess. Then they wrap me in the Villain *special* and cart me downtown.

The "villain special" is a restrictive outfit that's sort of like a turtleneck cocoon, made of a rubbery material, that they vacuum pack us in when we arrive at the Capital County Jail. It's even got a way to block the abilities of some of my former colleagues. Not sure how it works, though. Science isn't my strong suit. There's a helmet part for some of us, but they don't give that to me, just a hood piece. I do, however, get a thing that straps over my mouth to prevent me from spitting. Not that I would—that would be gross and rude.

Sitting in the special is hot and uncomfortable at the best of times, but on these stupid metal interrogation seats, it's horrible. I can't find a good position, and I can't rock around too much because I'll fall off. I'm a wobbly rubber worm. Embarrassing. So, I sit in the little room and wait for whoever is going to ask me about the stupid fucking graffiti. All of this over doodles. I can't fucking believe it.

Every time someone comes in—none of whom have been anyone associated with this graffiti so far—I ask for a lawyer, but they ignore me. Finally, a cop that actually has something to do with why I'm here comes in, and when he does, I can tell he's going to be a prick. Not that I expect anything else from Capital City's finest.

He slams a thick folder on the dirty table and stares at me. I don't say anything. When he realizes I know better than to talk first—at least this cop is smart—he starts in on me.

"Resisting arrest, huh? So eager to go back to rehab already."

"Lawyer." That's all I'm gonna say.

"Oh, you're one of those." He rolls his eyes. "We're just having a conversation, honey."

"Lawyer."

"Sure is late at night. Probably hard to get a lawyer. Better to just get this over with now."

He smells like coffee, and it's just reminding me how thirsty I am, which makes me angrier and less likely to cooperate. I don't even like coffee.

"Lawyer."

"Listen, sweetheart—"

The door behind me swings open.

"You gotta be fucking kidding me," the cop mumbles.

"Hello to you, too, Officer Powell!" a cheery voice says from behind me. "And hello to you too, Ms.... Lima?"

"Yes."

The man sits in the other shitty seat next to me. I turn my head as best I can to watch as he sets his briefcase on the table. He looks pretty put together for it being so late at night.

"I'm Mark Rivers. I'll be Ms. Lima's lawyer." He turns to look at me and smiles. A lawyer should not have so many freckles. "If that's alright, of course."

"Fine."

"Alright. Love the enthusiasm." He *winks* at me before turning to face the cop again. "So, what were you saying, officer?"

**

They had nothing on me because I didn't do anything. The footage from the officer's body cam proves I wasn't resisting either.

"Thanks. Was super sweaty in there," I mumble as the anxious, gloved officer undoes the last of my restraints. "Don't touch your eyes before you take off your gloves. Wouldn't want you to go blind or anything. Would be a shame."

"Ugh." The cop jerks away quickly as the suit falls to the floor. I shimmy out of it and stretch my arms wide. The cop steps further back. "Just leave that there on the floor, and someone will toss it."

"Whatever," I say, waving my hand at him dismissively.

I turn to my new lawyer and sigh as he hands me his business card. It's the first time in my adult life that I've been in public wearing nothing but leggings and a tank top. If I didn't have the whole weird face thing, I'd look like a normal person. Hmm, maybe I could even pass for some kind of Mashie.

"I don't suppose you have a way to help me get home, do you? I don't have my phone, wallet, or anything to cover my skin with. Going out in public is gonna be rough." I cross my arms and raise a brow.

"Unless you don't mind me bumping into some people. Leaving a trail of bodies on my walk home would give these pigs an actual reason to bring me in. They might even thank me."

"Well, you're in luck." He pulls his keys out of his suit jacket and gives them a little jingle. "You're my last case for the night, and my car seats are easy to clean. Let's get you home."

He walks over to the desk, knocks on the plexiglass, and smiles a toothy smile. The officer behind it looks at the lawyer as if he'd like to feed him those teeth.

"My client is going to need your finest lost and found clothing items, please," he says.

"Get your own shit, Rivers," the cop says, to no one's surprise.

Making no attempt to change my facial expression from its blank default, I grab my own ass, turn to the line of chairs in the waiting room, and loudly say, "Oh man, I think I broke my ass bone. I'd better lie down on these chairs. Oh my, I wonder if they changed the rules from the last time I was here about how the person working the front desk has to wipe down the chairs and tables in the lobby at night. Ow, ouch, my sweaty, poisonous ass."

"Alright, hold on," the cop shouts, slamming a stapler onto his desk as he stands. "Keep your ass and anything else off my chairs."

A few minutes later, a little window off to the side opens, and the cop shoves a bundle of fabric through it. I put on the dirty, oversized gray raincoat, dirtier gold lamé track pants, black winter gloves, and white sneakers.

"Now, fuck off," the cop snaps.

The lawyer makes a heart shape with his hands.

"Thank you, officer."

"Thanks." I salute him and start booking it toward the exit. As we're entering the parking garage, I see a clock above the door. "Is that the correct time?"

The lawyer checks his watch, then unlocks the door to his car.

"That's it. Four A.M. You were in there a while before I could get to you. Sorry."

I tug open the car door and slide in.

"Seatbelt, please, then your address," the lawyer says in a singsong voice.

I ramble off my address, then I click the seatbelt on, close my eyes, and lean back into the seat.

"Fuck. I'm supposed to start my first day at work today, and I'm gonna be late. I barely got the job as it is. There's no way they'll keep me on now."

"Well, can you call and tell them you'll be late? I can drop you off there instead."

"The store doesn't answer the phones until after opening. I have to be there two hours *before* it opens. I can't just go places unprepared either because of my—" I wave my arms up and down my body, "—situation. So that I don't kill everybody or whatever."

"I suppose that's important. How about you go up to your apartment, get ready as fast as you can, then we get you to work. I'll go in with you and explain what happened. If they fire you, at least you did the best you could. Sound good?"

I turn to him and inspect his face for signs of an ulterior motive. He glances at me and asks, "Why are you squinting?"

"Why are you being so nice?"

"Oh, that. I didn't choose to be a public defender for the money or free time—both of those are shit. I did it because I believe in rehabilitation. Giving people a chance to start over. If we can't get you working, that's gonna be a lot harder for you to do. I've got some free time this morning so..." He shrugs.

"Alright. I don't really have another choice, I guess."

"Ah, doesn't everyone dream of being someone's last resort?" He laughs. "I'll take it. Anyway, while I'm waiting for you, this will give me a chance to answer the emails I've been avoiding."

"Okay. I don't have to feel entirely indebted then."

"Nope. No debt owed. I do this out of the goodness of my heart. And a shitty paycheck from the government." He grins as he pulls up to my building. "I'll be right here, suffering in my inbox. Take your time."

"Thanks." I hustle into the dirty brick building as he opens his laptop.

I get ready faster than I have in a very long time. There's body powder on the front of my hoodie, and my hair is still half wet, but I'm out the door in less than forty minutes. That may seem like ages to a lot of people, but for me, it's practically an instant.

"Okay. I'm ready," I say as I slide back into the passenger seat.

"Fantastic. Though I miss the gold pants," he says as he sticks his laptop back into its spot in the backseat. "Now, where to?"

"Waljean's on Prospect Place."

"I know that location well. Here we go."

It's not a long drive, but it would have taken a lot longer on the bus. When we get there, Milly is unlocking the front doors. She smiles and waves when she sees the lawyer—it looks like they know one another—but when she notices me, her expression quickly changes.

"Two hours is well past acceptable, Tabitha," she says as we step into the store.

"I'm sorry," I say quietly.

The lawyer steps between the two of us. "That's the reason I'm here today, Milly. Perhaps we can head to the break room."

Milly's frown remains in place, but she nods and heads toward the back, both of us following. Once back there, the lawyer starts his defense.

"It wasn't her fault."

"She brought a lawyer to defend her tardiness?"

"I offered to come. This is a special circumstance. She was falsely accused of a crime—with no evidence or even reason to believe she was the one responsible in the first place—and held overnight at the station. Tabitha wanted to be here, and intends to be here, on time for her shifts. Right, Tabitha?"

"Absolutely."

"So, Milly, I believe you should give her a chance to start fresh without this late shift counting against her. What do you say?"

Milly sighs and pulls a badge and lanyard out of her pocket.

"Come on, Tabitha. Let's take your employee photo."

"Thank you, Milly!" He turns to me for a high five.

I look him up and down before poking the center of his palm with one gloved finger. He laughs and shakes his head.

"Thanks, Milly," I say.

Milly takes my photo, prints it out, and slips it into the plastic cover on the badge attached to the lanyard. "There you are, you're officially ready to go."

I slide it over my head and admire myself in the break room mirror.

The lawyer turns to Milly. "Can I walk to the back room with you guys so I can see my brother before I leave?"

"Of course," she says.

I raise an eyebrow at him but don't say anything else. No questions allowed here.

We all head back, Milly pointing things out to me as we go. When we arrive at the big double doors, she holds up a hand for the lawyer to stop, then she pokes her head inside and shouts, "Henry! Your brother is here to see you!"

Both eyebrows raise this time.

"Your brother is the Mashie?" I ask.

He frowns. "Is that a problem?"

"Of course not. I know my history with—but *I'm* not like that. I was *never* like that."

The little bit of goodwill built up between us shuts down. As soon as someone puts me on the same level as Darkiss, it sours things. I pull my hood further forward, hiding my face entirely, and cross my arms tightly around my body.

"Tabitha, I'm sorry. It's just so many people judge him for—"

The double doors swing open and out comes my grinning co-worker. His face is red from exertion, sweat coats his brow, and his ginger hair is sticking up in all directions. The one white streak in his hair sticks to his forehead. There's dust all over his "Mitochondria is the Powerhouse of the Cell" t-shirt. His tail slaps into the display of soup next to him, knocking several cans to the floor. Such a mess compared to his brother that it almost makes me smile.

"Howdy, Mark. Didn't expect you this morning. What's—" His eyes widen, and his grin grows when the lawyer pokes his thumb in my direction. "Do you two know each other?"

"Besties," I mumble. "Can I start my shift now?"

Milly claps her hands. "Yes! Let's go! We have a lot to do. I'm going to need to know why you're covered in dust, Henry. Though I'm afraid of the answer."

Henry runs forward to slap *Mark* a high five before running back to the double doors and waving goodbye.

I go to work without saying anything. I don't think the lawyer—*Mark*—permanently fucked things up, but...I don't know. I don't like it when people assume I'm a bad person.

Then again, some assumptions might be fair, considering my past. I did murder over a dozen people, and I was the sidekick of a genocidal maniac. It could be hard to look past that.

Chapter Six

Henry

"Wait, so was Mark your lawyer?" I ask Tabitha once Milly leaves. Took her forever to train Tabitha in all the technical stuff. I was itching to talk to her the whole time.

"Yep." She continues to fetch the boxes from the highest shelf. My tall Queen. Goddess of the sky.

"He's a great lawyer. Super passionate about helping the little guys. Not that you're a little guy. I mean, you're tall, but that's not what I mean either. He likes helping people who need it." *Wow, real suave.*

"Nice." Champion of the concise replies, she is.

Cringing at my own awkwardness, I squeeze the Lumberman brand paper towels to my chest. As far as superheroes go, Lumberman's not that great. Literally, his superpower is splitting trees. *Big whoop.* But he really did find the perfect marketing opportunity. Good for him.

I elbow her in the boot. "If you two ever need to team up for an exciting investigation, let me know. I'm in."

"Yeah, okay," Tabitha says, giving me the side-eye—well, downwards eye—then thankfully moving on. "It was nice that he helped me with Milly. I forgot to say thanks. So, tell him I did, or whatever."

I perk up and throw the paper towels a little too aggressively to the side so I can search my pockets for my phone. *Damn you, pants pockets with your plentiful hiding space!*

"Well, you could tell him yourself. I'll give you his number, and you could text him."

"I already have his number. In case I get in trouble again." She shrugs. "Hopefully, I don't, but the cops don't like me, so who knows? I don't know, I don't want to text him for other shit and bother him."

"Well, I can give you my number." I very intentionally avoid looking at her, so that I don't have to see it if she laughs at me. To keep my hands busy, I open a box of...lube. Okay.

"Why?"

"Oh, uh, in case you need me to cover for you. At work. Or something. Anything."

She looks at the—frankly, flamboyantly packaged—bottle of lube I'm holding and squints. *Shit.*

"Are you messing with me?"

"What? No!" I look at her now and find her watching my expression closely. I feel like a mouse in a dark room coming upon the yellow glow of a cat's eyes. Absolutely frozen in terror. "Why would you think that?"

Her expression softens, and now she doesn't look like she could kill me. She's looking at me like she thinks I'm a fucking idiot. Which is much worse.

"Are you serious? Do you know how many Mashies have tried to take their anger at Darkiss out on me?" She descends from the ladder carrying a box far heavier than I'd ever be able to and drops it in front of me.

Oh, right.

"Fuck. I'm sorry. That's not my intention, though, believe me. Just being friendly."

A jingling sound comes from Tabitha's direction. She pulls her phone from her hoodie and silences the alarm.

"It's time for my break."

"Oh, let me join you. I still have to take mine."

"I want to be alone. No offense."

"Oh." I can feel my tail droop. When did that come out again? Damn thing was supposed to be taped down. "That's fine. I'll take mine after you."

"Okay. Thanks for understanding."

When she leaves, I tape my tail down *again* and get my mopey ass back to work. There's a lot to do today, so the last few hours fly by.

When we're clocking out, I ask her if she wants a ride home, but she insists she's fine with the bus. As we reach the exit, however, she stops me with a, "Hold on."

"What's up?" I ask, looking around to see if something's wrong.

Without looking me in the eye, she pulls out her phone and unlocks it. "What's your number? Just in case I ever need you for something. Or anything."

In my excitement, I recite my number so fast that she has to have me repeat it twice. Once she's got it locked in, she says, "Okay," and then she's out the door.

"Yes!" I give myself a congratulatory high-five.

There's a pat on my back, and I look down to see Milly walking past me on her way out, muttering, "Such a strange man."

When I get home, I shower, eat some soup, and then look around online to see if anything exciting is happening tonight. The answer is a big no. It looks like a lot of downtown has been closed last minute to prepare for Honor Man's something or other. Mark is doing family stuff until later. Everyone else works this time of day. *Ugh.*

I find myself back on the Poison Princess forum. People are wondering what she's up to, looking for updates. They're talking about her arrest last night. I desperately want to say something about work, but I can't—no way am I going to out my identity on this thing. With a sigh, I close the site. It holds no excitement for me any longer. Now that I actually know her in person, there isn't really a point to a fan forum.

Now what to do? There's not even anything on TV. What a boring day.

Finally, even though I try to resist it, I pick up my phone and wind up where I find myself too often: the SuperFuckersOnline app.

Yeah. I know it's pathetic, but I can't help it—I've got a thing for powered people. A full-on kink. The SFO app matches regular humans and Mashies, with Superheroes and (rehabbed) Villains, who are looking to hook up. No strings. You have to sign a form saying you won't expose anyone, due to the sensitive nature of the identities. It's pretty controversial, actually. But *fuck*, it's the only place I can get what I like.

I set my currently inactive profile to active, then start swiping. Capital City has the most Heroes and Villains of any place in the world, of any gender or sexuality, and today the app is on fire. We don't get to see names from our side, and the Heroes and Villains do the initial messaging. We can only swipe based on their basic profile information. But soon I get a match and a message.

SPH1: Looking when?

Me: Tonight.

SPH1: Into? More pics?

Me: Need someone strong. Powerful. My place.

I send him some pics of my, uh, *assets.*

SPH1: I've got strength, believe me. Something big and powerful for that ass.

Not the most creative messaging on our parts, but this type of situation does not call for poetry. The picture he sends me back has me clenching in my seat, and that's what matters for an afternoon fling. I send him my address, and shortly after, my front door buzzes.

A very large, muscular man, whom I recognize as the Superhero Sailor Photon, arrives. Just my type.

About an hour and a half later, he's gone, and I'm washing glowing cum off of my ass, my face, and my ceiling. I whistle a merry tune as I contemplate taking an ibuprofen or eight, and scrub away the neon jizz.

Superheroes are so cool.

Chapter Seven

Tabitha.

"You're gonna have to pay for this. I'm sorry, Tabitha," my landlord says as she screws the new metal plate onto my front door. "This is beyond normal wear and tear."

"It's not like I asked the cops to break it. They had no reason to smash the knob off an already open door."

"I'm sure there was a good reason."

I point to the stove. "What was the reason for breaking the dials off the stove?"

"Are you sure that was them? Doesn't seem like something they'd do." She shrugs when she catches my open-mouthed look of disbelief. "I'm serious. Never had a problem with the police here."

I take in her perfectly normal beige skin, brown hair, and green eyes. The fact that people let her into their homes every day, no questions asked. I'm not surprised her experience with law enforcement was different from mine.

"It'll be fifty to fix the door—I had most of the stuff already—but it's two hundred to fix the stove. I'll need that with your rent this month, Tabitha."

"Two hundred and fifty dollars?" Numbers fly around in my head. I try to arrange them in a way that will make the amount I'll earn in my first paycheck cover rent plus this new bill, but it's not going to work. "I can't do that, Lisa."

"That's just how it is." She wipes her hands on her jeans as she stands, then picks up her tools. "You know where to find me if you need anything else."

I watch her walk to the end of the hall and down the stairs. Ms. Lee walks by, toward her place, glancing back at Lisa, before adjusting her glasses. She clears her throat, raises one speckled, arthritic hand to the side of her mouth, and leans toward me as she passes by.

"They used to execute landlords back in my day. Can't say I blame them," she says quietly, nods, then unlocks her door.

I bark out a surprised laugh before I close my own door. Didn't expect that.

Alright, what now? I pull out my phone and flop my sad ass straight onto my futon, belly-first. *Fuck.* This is going to take some deep digging into the hellish depths of my email.

There are a lot of people who are interested in me because of the whole Villain thing, and they're willing to pay money for different things. I've taken the easiest offers already—the interview with O'Leary, for example. All that's left are the less enticing options.

I open my account and ignore the folder marked "Will Definitely Send Me Back to Jail" and open the one marked "Legally Questionable." That's all I really have left at this point. After moving a few over to the jail folder, I find one possibility. I'd get a good chunk of change out of it, plus it's one of the few from a reputable source. Yes, it's an "adult media" corporation, but reputable, nonetheless.

The only problem is I'm not sure if what they want would break the terms of my release. To get out of prison, we had to sign a pretty long agreement about how we would behave publicly. I don't want to do something that will get me back into solitary, talking to the rats.

Fuck it, I'll ask for help. I'm trying to be a new person, after all. I open the contacts list in my phone and stare at the name. Butterflies crawl around in my guts. *Mark Rivers*. Alright, well, I'm not going to waste the few free resources I've been given. Here we go. I press the number and wait while it rings. I'm sure it will go to voicemail and then he—

"Hello, Tabitha. How are you?" he answers, a solid note of curiosity in his voice.

"Oh, uh, hi. I'm okay. Not in jail."

"That's what I like to hear. What can I do for you then?"

"I'm sorry to bother you, it's just I had a legal question, and I was hoping you could help me. If you don't want to, that's fine."

"Tabitha, it's alright. Henry just arrived, though, so if you'd like to wait for a private conversation—"

"It's fine, it's just a quick question."

"Go ahead then."

"Okay. When I got arrested, the cops broke some stuff in my house, and I have to pay my landlord at the end of the month to fix it. I don't have extra money to pay her. It's not like I can just sell my stuff either, because it's all contaminated. But anyway, I got an offer to do some, uh, *adult modeling*. The thing is, they want me to wear my old gear in the photos. So, my question is, would that violate the terms of the Villain rehabilitation release program?"

There's a lot of shuffling noise on the other end before Mark returns with a response.

"If your terms are anything like the others I've worked with who had costumed personas, then I would recommend against it. Especially considering how well-known your costume was and how tied in your appearance is to your Villain identity. Doing sexual imagery in costume could be seen as glorifying, or positively promoting, that identity, which is definitely against the terms of your release." He pauses for a moment when he hears me sigh. "I'm sorry, Tabitha. I'm surprised you still have those clothes. I would have thought they'd made you throw them out like they did the other former Villains."

"Oh, I had a ton of copies of my look stashed all over. I guess I can't ever wear them again. Might as well just throw them away."

A muffled voice shouts from the other end of the line, "No! God, no!"

There are more shuffling sounds before Mark speaks again. "Ah, you never know. How much money do you need anyway?"

"Two hundred and fifty dollars. Which might as well be a million because I can't pay it either way." I kick a pillow across the room in frustration and then immediately feel bad; it's not the pillow's fault I'm broke. *Sorry, pillow.*

"Capital City police are *supposed* to reimburse people for things like that. In practice, however, they rarely do. I may be able to help you, though. There's a fund I have access to. It's for people who might not easily find a helping hand when they need one. I have a feeling you're one of those people."

I can't help but snort a laugh. Aside from Milly and Mark, helping hands have been virtually nonexistent my entire life. Well, unless you count Darkiss.

"I can send something along with Henry. Is that alright?"

Well, damn.

"That sounds really good, Mark. Thank you."

When we hang up, I have to sit and stare at the phone for a minute to recover. It's a really new feeling for me—getting help just because someone *wants* to help. There have *always* been strings attached to everything in life, and this feels so... I don't even *know* how it feels. I'm too afraid to fully appreciate it because I'm still waiting for the other shoe to drop.

The last time I thought someone was going to do something really nice for me was when I trusted the couple who took me from the group home. I really thought I was going to a loving family that time. *Nope.* Who knew the government was out there scooping up kids and turning them into hybrid freaks?

Well, they *were*. Not sure they are anymore after I killed all their "expert" scientists. Maybe they've hired new ones. They'd better hope another one of their experiments doesn't get free, if that's the case.

I suppose Darkiss freeing us from the facility was another nice thing. He didn't *have* to help me track down all the scientists who tortured me, but he did it out of the goodness of his heart. Everyone has a good side.

Since then, though, things have been downhill.

The next day, Milly gives me my very own sticker gun. Some of the night shift people were being assholes about using one I may have touched—even though they were assured I wore gloves—so now there is a Tabitha exclusive. It's covered in neon green discount stickers, so everyone knows it's just for me. Honestly, I'm not mad about it. I love putting stickers on shit. It's relaxing. Having my own gun gives me a reason to find more things that need stickers, too.

Then, surprisingly, it's when I'm sticking "final clearance" tags on cans of pineapple ravioli that the most unexpected twist of my life occurs.

"Ka-bam," I mumble to myself as another neon green sticker adheres to the can.

Each time I click the gun, I can't help but say that quietly. Not sure why. It's just come out naturally the, oh, thousand times I've stickered something today.

"Ka-bam."

"You're so freaking weird." Henry laughs. "Every time I walk by you today, I hear your little 'ka-bam.'"

"Stop listening so hard," I grumble.

"I can't help it. My hearing is excellent." He props his elbow on a pallet of toilet paper rolls. "My a lot of things are excellent."

"Wow, okay," I laugh. "Thanks for sharing."

"Yes, I am excellent at sharing, that's one of the 'a lot of things'." He pops the collar of his shirt with a smug look. One of the packages of toilet paper falls off the pallet.

"Oh, gee. I'll have to break out my swooning skills." I roll my eyes and continue stickering my cans. "Ka-bam."

Henry straightens up. "Well, you know, in case you want to practice swooning, I'm open to that sort of thing."

"Open to swooning?" I raise my eyebrow at him. "Ka-bam."

"Open to anything." Henry's cheeks turn slightly pink. "In case you're ever wondering."

"Is that something you *want* me to wonder about, Henry?"

Now I feel my cheeks heating up. He can't be seriously flirting. I mean, he knows I'll kill him if I touch him, right? Whatever. It's just friendly jokes.

"I certainly would not be opposed to it, Tabitha."

A smile tugs at the corners of my lips as I tuck my head against my shoulder, attempting to hide my expression. Out of habit, I reach back to grab my hood, but as I do, I lose my hold on the sticker gun. When I try to catch it, I overcorrect my balance. My foot slips off the ladder.

"Shit!" I shout as I tumble down.

The fall doesn't last long, and I never make it to the floor. I catch my sticker machine in one hand—and am surprised to find my other arm wrapped around the neck of a Mashie. An opossum Mashie who looks much more handsome up close than I thought he would.

Henry holds me cradled like a baby in his arms. A very tall baby. For a second, I look into his bright hazel eyes and feel like a dainty little damsel. He smiles down at me, the lights above creating an angelic corona around him. *Wow,* he has even more freckles than his brother.

"You gotta be more careful," he says. "Not that I mind having you in my arms. Pretty fond of it, actually."

I become very aware of his grip on me. *It's okay. Don't panic. He's not touching my skin.*

Except... wait, is he?

My body stiffens, and my breathing stops, when I feel the touch above my boot. It's just a soft graze at first, barely noticeable. My eyes shoot down and see my pant leg has ridden up. He's not touching me, though. *Maybe I imagined it.* I start to breathe again.

Just as I start to pull away from Henry, his now-familiar pink tail slithers into view. It wraps around my boot, the tip creeping upward toward the tiny sliver of exposed skin.

"No!" I scream, shoving him away. "No, please!"

"Whoa, hey. Whatever I did, I'm sorry. Seriously," he says, confusion on his face as he sets me on the ground.

"Let me go! Hurry!" I beg as I pull my leg away from him, but his tail yanks me back.

Henry only then notices his tail sliding under my pants leg.

"Oh, shit!" he says as he quickly unfurls it from around my boot and whips it back.

"We have to get you to a hospital. Please don't die." I fumble for my phone, my stupid gloves making everything ten times harder to do when I'm panicking.

Henry holds his tail to the fluorescent light to inspect it, then looks back at me. "How am I supposed to feel? Because I feel fine."

"Pain? Hallucinations? Not fine!" I finally get my phone out.

"Huh. I don't think it's working on me. Has that ever happened before?" He sticks out his tongue and, like some lunatic with a death wish, *licks* his tail.

"What are you doing? Stop that!" When I slap his tail away from his hand, I drop my phone. "Dammit! And no, it hasn't happened before."

"Tabitha, I don't think it's working. Maybe you stopped being poisonous." He shrugs.

I glare at him. "I very highly doubt that."

"Then it doesn't work on me."

"I doubt that as well." I crouch in front of Henry and search for my now-missing phone. "There's some other explanation. There has—"

Fucking stupid Henry, with his death wish, leans until he's so close to me I could count his amber-colored eyelashes, and pushes my hair behind my ear. Instinctually, I grab his other hand in self-defense. He seems to take that in a romantic way, because he chooses that moment to close the gap between us. Very softly, on my cheekbone where the yellow patch meets the blue patch, he places a kiss. Then he steps back and continues on.

Like he didn't just completely shatter everything I know about my future.

I'm stunned into silence. Smiling the whole while, he finds my phone for me, then my sticker machine, and hands them both to me. He scoops me under the arms and pulls me to a standing position.

"Go on now. You've still got horribly-flavored ravioli to put stickers on. I've gotta go back to work being excellent at things." When I still don't move, he jiggles my hand holding the sticker gun. "Ka-bam, remember?"

"Ka-bam."

With that, he heads to the loading dock and returns to his daily routine, while I stare at his back for a solid two minutes before I can even think straight.

He can touch me.

Chapter Eight

Henry

The "fund" Mark referenced isn't an official charity; it's just something a handful of kind citizens put together for emergencies. For people in situations like Tabitha's, it's way too easy for a minor debt to cause major problems. Our system is not set up to help them at all. Little issues can snowball quickly, destroying their chance at a new life. A few hundred dollars might not mean much to some people, but it can be life-saving to others.

At the end of the workday, I wait for Tabitha to finish her project so I can give her the money. She declined my offer to help her finish up, so I clocked out. Now, I'm bored and hungry. I'll get some chocolate. We have plenty of that here. I mosey up front and check out the candy.

"Hello, Henry!" Milly greets cheerfully from behind the front counters.

"Oh, hello there! What are you doing at the registers?"

"People are calling in sick a lot lately. Looks like I'm working overtime this week."

I slap two chocolate bars and a pack of red licorice on the counter. "Ick. Sorry about that, Milly."

Milly waves off my comment and rings up the candy. I glance at the television playing overhead, and I'm surprised by the captions.

WEDDING OF THE CENTURY?

HONOR MAN MARRIES CAPITAL CITY WOMAN.

CEREMONY WILL BE OPEN TO ALL.

"Didn't expect that," I say, pointing to the TV.

Milly glances back and shrugs. "I'm just excited to find out who it is he's marrying. I heard it's just a regular lady. That's kind of fun."

"Huh. He always seemed mysterious. Weird that it's going to be a public thing." I pay for the candy, then go to the break room to wait for Tabitha.

I get through the licorice and one bar of chocolate before the door flies open. Tabitha stomps toward the employee lockers without acknowledging me. I clear my throat and spin my chair in her direction.

"Hello there."

"Hey." Tabitha waves, then tugs her purse from the tiny locker.

I wave my candy bar-occupied hand at her and reach for my wallet with the other. "Don't leave yet, hold on. Let me give you—"

"Can you drive me? With my luck, I'll get robbed." She crosses her arms, holding her purse tightly against her. "It's okay if not."

"It's not a problem at all, I don't mind. I should take you home every day. Might as well." I shrug. "It's not far."

"Oh, no. That's okay. I'm fine."

"Offer stands if you change your mind."

We head out, wave bye to Milly on the way, then get into my car. She has to scoot her seat back to fit her long legs, then gives me her address to plug into my GPS. We're just turning onto the street when my phone rings. It's Mark.

"One sec." I hit the accept call on my dashboard. "Hey, Mark. I'm driving home."

"Alright. Just wanted to make sure Tabitha got the funds," he says.

"Hi, Mark," she chimes in.

"Oh, hello, Tabitha," he says, sounding surprised. "How are you?"

"I'm fine. Thanks."

"I touched Tabitha's skin," I blurt out.

Don't really know why. I can't ever keep things from Mark.

Tabitha's head snaps to the side. "What the hell, Henry?"

"Are you okay?" Mark sounds panicked. "Do you need help? What's going on?"

"I'm fine. That's the thing—I'm totally, completely fine!" I look at Tabitha and grin. "Right?"

"Watch out!" Tabitha shouts.

I look back just in time to veer out of the way of a little old cat Mashie woman crossing the street. *Fuck, that was close.* My heart races, and I shake my head to get my focus back.

"What do you mean you're fine? Was there a doctor? I need to know what happened, Henry," Mark insists.

"He just... didn't die," Tabitha says from next to me. "It's weird. He had no reaction. It's never happened before."

"We can't tell anyone about this," he says. "I'm serious. You *cannot* tell anyone."

"Uh, okay." I glance at Tabitha. "But why?"

"How do you think I got this way? I wasn't born with this affliction, Henry."

"I've read some stuff online about secret government testing. I thought it might be conspiracy nonsense, but Mark told me that in his line of work he's seen proof that—"

"Excuse me, I'm certain you don't mean to say I've ever broken client confidentiality or—" Mark cuts in.

"Don't worry, Mark, I would never say that. I'm only saying I've heard some credible theories about Tabitha, her crew, and some kind of fucked-up mad science shit."

"Fucked-up is right. And Mark is right about us not telling anyone you're immune," Tabitha says firmly. "You're the *only* one immune to my poison. I've seen what happens when they find someone who can counter a Villain's ability. They'll do whatever it takes to get that for themselves. No matter what it does to you."

I pull up to the curb in front of Tabitha's building. She gets out of the car before I'm even fully parked and stomps toward her door.

"Gotta go, Mark." I slap the end call button.

Fuck. I park at a sloppy angle and hurry out, jogging behind her. She fumbles at the lock with her keys, cursing her gloves.

"Hey, what's wrong?" I ask. "You seem upset."

"No shit," she snaps as she finally twists the lock, then yanks the door outward.

I follow a huffing and puffing Tabitha into the building. When she looks back and sees me following her, she growls low in an annoyed way, but doesn't tell me to stop.

"No, but seriously, are you okay?" I persist.

Tabitha unlocks the door to her apartment and swings it wide without answering. I enter, locking it behind us. Tabitha squints at me.

"Don't touch anything. Nothing has even been wiped down. There could be traces of poison anywhere. Everywhere. Just don't. Okay?"

"Okay." I flop onto her futon.

"I just said don't touch anything!"

"Hey, I have to sit!"

Her nostrils flare, and I can tell she's trying not to commit an act of violence against me. *Thank you, my darling. I like you too.*

"We can try to figure this out together," I say. "Maybe if we know why I'm immune, that'll be helpful."

"Whatever," Tabitha mumbles.

I pull out my phone and start typing. "I'll search for people with dart frog immunities and see if something comes up, maybe, I don't know."

I type for a few seconds before my tail slips out and bangs loudly against the tabletop. That gives me an idea.

"What about an opossum? Is there some connection there at all?" I ask.

Tabitha tilts her head in wary intrigue. "Not sure. Check it out."

I type rapidly. Tabitha cranes her neck slightly, trying to sneak a peek at my phone.

"And there it is! Some opossums are immune to dart frog poison. Looks like being a Mashie paid off for once." I grin at Tabitha before noticing her still-hard expression. I touch her knee, briefly, and chase her eyes for contact. "If they happen to come for me, I can offer up that information so they don't have to torture me to figure it out. If that's what you're worried about."

Tabitha lets out a long breath, as if she'd been holding it in this whole time.

"Mark is right, though. It's still risky to let anyone know. I can't let anyone go through anything even close to what I did if I can help it."

I touch her knee again, a little longer this time.

"I promise. I'm not interested in being a government science experiment. Okay? All I want to do is spend time with you." I rest my fingertips on her knee, waiting to see if she brushes them away; she doesn't. "I really like you, Tabitha."

Her expression changes. A stillness comes over her, no emotion displayed through her mouth, her brows, the corners of her eyes. But in the liquid black of the eyes themselves, something even darker stirs.

"I killed the only person I've ever kissed," she says matter-of-factly. "When I was still a teenager. His name was John. He was also in the institute. I kissed him, and he died. The way you have your hand on my knee? That makes me feel as if you want to kiss me someday. So, I think it's only fair that you should know about John."

Okay, now we're getting somewhere. My chest feels like it's going to burst, but I think that's probably fine.

"I do want to kiss you someday, and I don't think it'll be the same thing as with the other guy," I assure her. "I doubt he, John, was part opossum. I'm sorry that happened, though. It must have been rough, especially for someone so young. I hate that you had to go through that."

Tabitha leans toward me, lips pressed in a thin line, brow lowered. Her eyes are shining brighter, and suddenly I'm nervous.

"I've killed a lot of people, Henry. The rest weren't accidents. I knew what would happen when I touched them, and I did it anyway. I'm not sorry, and in the same situation I'd do it again." Her eyes open so wide I feel as if someone could fall into them and drown. She leans closer, and for the first time since I've met her, I lean away. "I've done awful things. Yes, I regret a couple of those things—John, for example—but what's important is that I *loved* doing *a lot* of them."

My heart feels like it's beating in my intestines and my throat at the same time as I continue to stare into the infinite depths of her amphibian predator's eyes.

"Why are you telling me this?"

"I'm telling you this, Henry, because you're talking to me as if I'm someone who just got out of jail for stealing candy. It's sweet, it is. I do like you, but the way you brush off potentially being taken away and tortured by the government is really concerning, though." She shakes her head when I offer up a dismissive wave and a cheeky grin. "See? You're risking everything for me—who I'm sure you'll hate once you get to know a single fact about me."

It's my turn to laugh— If only she knew how much I know about her past. So many late-night deep dives.

Tabitha gives me a sharp look. I smooth out my expression.

"I want to know as much as you want to tell me. I'm not asking you to marry me. Let's just hang out. See where things go. I promise not to make things weird at work if things go south."

Tabitha groans in frustration as she pushes her fingers back through her hair, but she's smiling while she does it. *Yes!*

"Okay. But no flirting at work. I want to keep my job. It's important to me. *Seriously*. Everything needs to be separate."

"Cross my heart." I make an X over my chest. "You won't even know I'm there unless you need help with something."

She looks me over as she nervously bites her bottom lip. Finally, she stands, turns her back to me, and pulls off her thick hoodie, so that she's wearing only a black t-shirt and her long gloves.

"And you have to scratch this itch between my shoulder blades. It's been bothering me all day, and I can't reach it. If you can touch me, then please be useful."

"Gladly."

I spring up and move much closer to her than strictly necessary. She lets out a long moan as I scratch her back. *Oh my god.*

"Yes, right there. That feels so good," she says.

"Is there anywhere else that needs attention? Any other itch I can scratch?" I press my front against her back.

Tabitha takes a sharp breath. I reach around her and drag my thumb across her bottom lip. She's so *soft*.

"I—I want to—" Tabitha can't seem to decide what to say. Though when she reaches back, holds onto my hips, and grinds her ass against my hardening cock, it gives me an idea of how she's feeling.

"Tell me what you want," I speak softly at the back of her neck, so close my lips brush her skin with each word. She closes her eyes, breathing quickly, her hips slowly rolling. "Anything for you, Princess."

Before I know anything has even gone wrong, I'm on the floor, clutching my stomach, and Tabitha has a boot pressed to my throat.

"You're a SuperFucker, aren't you?" she snarls. "That's all this is. You don't like *me*. Are you going to sell this story to the tabloids? Or is this just to report to some forum? You people are so fucking sick."

Oh, shit. As I struggle to pull the boot from my neck, concerned for my life, she proceeds to ignore me entirely.

"There are plenty of Villains who fuck fetishists consensually, did you know that?" She scoffs. "Who am I kidding? Of course you do. This is so screwed up. You know, I may not be able to poison you, but I know a lot of other fun tricks."

"Tabitha," I squeeze out, "This is all a misunderstanding."

"A misunderstanding? Calling me *Princess*, of all things? Sure, total coincidence. If I download that SuperFuckersOnline app right now, can you tell me you won't have a profile on it?"

My stomach sinks. I sure as shit do have one.

"It's not like that," I say, my breath getting weaker.

Tabitha doesn't buy it. Her face turns red with anger as she points to the front door. She finally steps off as she stomps toward the entrance.

"Get the fuck out. *Now*," she growls.

Gasping as I stand, I try one more time to plead my case. "I really want to explain—"

"OUT!"

I do as she asks. As I'm leaving, however, I leave the three hundred dollars cash on her coffee table without saying anything. It's money I promised her, regardless of whether we get along. Thankfully, she doesn't try to reject the offer.

An ancient woman in the hallway looks between Tabitha and me and says, "Sweetie, I have a gun if you need me to shoot him."

"Not today, Ms. Lee. Thanks." Then Tabitha slams the door behind me and locks it.

***

When I get home, I take a shower, then I call Mark. My voice is scratchy from being squashed. He insists on coming over. We sit in front of the TV and play cards like we always do when we need to talk about something serious.

"Alright, let it out. Why am I here?"

"I think we like each other. Well, it seemed like it."

"And then what?"

"I accidentally called her Princess, and she called me a SuperFucker."

"Well, you are, so..."

"Not the point. Then she elbowed me in the gut and stomped on my throat."

"I thought you liked it rough—"

"Not in the bad way, Mark. Keep up."

"Sorry, sorry."

"She pretty much thinks I'm a fetishizing piece of shit that wants to sell her story to the media." I cough and rub the darkening bruise on my neck. *Wow, she fucked me up.* "It just sucks. I really fucking like her. Getting to know her these last few days has been crazy. Everything has been so shitty since the Mash-Up, and finally I have something to look forward to every day."

He nods for me to go on.

"And I know that, yes, I have the whole kink. The fact that I've had a crush on her public persona for years is also true. I can see how that would be weird for her, and I will have to tell her eventually. But that's not why I like her. Maybe initially, but not now. The Princess thing just came out. *Fuck.* "I drop my cards on the table and rub my eyes with the heels of my hands. "How am I gonna fix this? *Can* I fix this?"

"I don't know, Henry. Maybe you can, maybe you can't. Whatever you do, though, don't annoy her at work. That's a sure-fire way to lose her."

I groan. "That's the only time I see her."

"You'll have to figure something else out, brother."

"I guess so."

Chapter Nine

Tabitha

I can't believe I was so stupid. For a moment, I thought he liked *me*. Just me. Stupid, stupid. What even is there to like about me anyway? Fuck, I'm nothing but a useless, unwanted, piece of—

No. I'm not going to spiral into self-loathing. Despite how shitty things might seem, the fact is, things are getting better for me. This is nothing. In fact, it's a good thing. I don't need anyone getting in my way. Right now, I can focus solely on improving my future. Alone.

Sitting down and finally taking off my boots relieves some of the tension in my body. I chuck them across the room so they're next to the front door where they're supposed to be. I don't remember much about my mother, but I know she and Darren had one thing in common—no wearing shoes in the house. I smirk at the memory of Darkiss lecturing four young Supervillains, all in costume, on household manners. The mental images sometimes seem truly surreal.

With a sigh, I shake off the past and focus on the present. I take out my phone and send a text to my landlord letting her know I have her money and that I'll send it in with my rent. There. More tension released, and one step closer to being back on track. Back to focusing on me. Alone. Yep.

An unwanted thought creeps in, one that drowns out all the others. *Was I being too quick to judge?*

I try to brush the thought away and go about my daily business, but the thought persists. *What if I'm wrong about him? I do like him...*

And what if I'm giving up my only chance to be with someone I can touch?

With a groan, I curl up on the futon, holding my phone close to my face. I stare at Henry's number and think.

Fuck it. By the time evening comes around, I can't handle thinking about it any longer. I'll send a message and get it over with.

If he tries to tell me he doesn't have one, then this is done. I'm not stupid. I could tell by the look on his face that he does, and I don't tolerate liars.

He doesn't reply at all, at least not for a while. After staring at my phone, waiting for the dots to appear, I give up and head to the fridge. I cut an apple into even slices, removing any trace of bruises, make a peanut butter sandwich with the peanut butter going all the way to the edges, and pour myself a glass of water. I finish all of it, wash my hands, then settle back onto the futon to read the news. It's close to bedtime before I get a response.

The first picture is a mirror selfie of him in a fairly tight white t-shirt and jeans. Admittedly, he looks good. He's not trying to hide that he's a Mashie—his tail is wrapped around his upper thigh, on full display—and his username is MashieFuckToy. I blink a few times at the spicy username before moving on to the next image.

It's a screenshot of his bio, which is not long.
Opossum Mashie.
31M. Bi.
Hook-ups only.
Treat me like a Villain.
The third image is his "unlocked" image, the private, nude one that only people he matches with can see—though he cropped out everything below the hip bones. How polite of him. For a moment, I'm distracted by his upper body. He's a little skinnier than I'm normally attracted to, but he pulls it off well. All in all, cute in a geeky way. Nothing on his profile seems too bad, I guess. Maybe he's sincere, after all.

But then, I spot the poster behind him, and that tiny spark of hope fizzles out. *A fucking Poison Princess poster.*

I start to type several different curses, erasing each one, then starting over, before ultimately growling in frustration. What am I supposed to say? There isn't anything aside from, "I told you I was right," and it's not like he doesn't obviously know that.

This was foolish. I shouldn't have texted. *Ugh*. Then, a text pops up.

Henry: From the dots indicating the many, many texts you've started and not sent, I have a feeling you've seen the poster.

Henry: Can we talk about it?

Me: What's there to say? It's exactly what I was worried about.

Me: It's a kink.

Me: Forget I messaged.

Henry: Yeah, it was, before I met you. Not anymore.

Me: Sure.

Henry: Ok, I'm still into the sex stuff, not gonna lie. The same reasons you turned me on before, still turn me on now. It's just that there's new stuff too.

> **Me:** This isn't helping.

Surprisingly, I get a text from someone else. This isn't a common occurrence for me. *Guess I'm Miss Popular tonight.* When I see who's on the other end of the second text, I laugh.

> **Mark:** He's an idiot, but I swear he really does like you.

> **Mark:** He came over to my house, acting quite pathetic and heartbroken. He's been here all evening. Tell him to go home, please.

I open my texts to Henry again.

> **Me:** Your brother thinks you're genuine.

> **Henry:** He's smart. Did you know he's a lawyer?

> **Me:** Haha, very funny.

> **Henry:** I'm funny. It's one of my many excellent qualities.

> **Me:** Not this again.

> **Me:** Don't think you'll distract me from the issue at hand.

Henry: Did you know opossums play dead to get predators to leave them alone?

Henry: (Did that distract you?)

Me: No.

Henry: Dang. Well, maybe we can get together and talk about it? I won't bother you at work, obviously.

Me: You better not!

Henry: I won't!

I bite my lip as I consider it. It's not like I won't be seeing him five days a week anyway. Couldn't hurt, right? *Ugh*, I'm such a pushover.

Me: Fine. Tomorrow at seven. Meet in front of my place.

Me: Bye.

Henry: Seven!

Hmm. Now I need to decide what we'll do. Something that will really let me get to know whether I can trust him.

The city lights peek through a hole in my curtain, projecting a perfect yellow circle on the opposite wall. It triggers the memory of a gold coin flashing in a woman's long, pale fingers. *I wonder if I still have her number.* I scroll down to the letter K in my contacts.

It's there—Klaire. A grin takes over my face. *Perfect.* She hates texts, so I call her to tell her my plan.

"Tabby, doesn't this whole thing seem a little complicated? You couldn't just have a heart-to-heart with him and try to trust your gut?" she says.

"*Pfft.* When has my gut ever been right? Besides, that's no fun."

I lie back, kick my feet up, and stretch. The last of the day's tension releases.

"You know it's true, Klaire—the best part of being a Supervillain are the overly elaborate plans."

Chapter Ten

Henry

She barely even looked at me all day while we worked. It was super awkward. The only way I got through without dropping to my knees and begging her to give me a chance was knowing I would see her tonight.

If things don't go well, I can always rethink the begging thing.

"Are you sure I look alright?" I ask Mark again.

"You look fine, like I told you already."

"But *trustworthy* fine?"

I'm wearing a nice blue shirt because I heard that blue makes people appear more confident and honest. Also, it looks nice on me.

"Very. I'd trust you not to eat my fries if I left them unattended."

I place my hand on his shoulder and offer him a pitying look.

"I'm sorry to tell you that I absolutely *would* steal your fries."

"I know, but you *look* like you wouldn't." He fixes my collar, pats my cheek, then pushes me out of his apartment door. "Now please, go away."

I panic all the way to Tabitha's, convinced she'll change her mind before I get there, but when I pull up to the curb, she's already there waiting. She's in all black, full hood, like always. It's past sunset, so I can't see her expression in the shadows. Hopefully, she's happy to see me. When I get out of the car, intending to open the door for her, she's already stomping my way, dead set on doing it herself.

"Come on," she says without so much as a *hello*. "Let's go."

"Oh, okay then. Lead the way," I say, getting back into the car as she slams the door. "Point the way, Tabitha."

"Go all the way south on Garfield. As far as you can go. Then we'll get out."

"That's—are you sure?"

That's not exactly the type of area you go to hang out with your friends. Well, I don't anyway.

"Yes," Tabitha says.

"Tabitha, I'm not sure we have the same idea of what kind of night this is going to be. I thought we were just gonna talk. I'm a little confused."

A little confused by the fact that we're headed to the freaking red-light district, for one. Pretty big mixed signals right there.

Tabitha looks back at me and squints. I both love and hate that squint. It's never been directed toward me in a positive way, but she just looks so darn cute.

"Don't get any funny ideas. We're just visiting a friend." She turns back around. "Not partaking of the kind of services you're thinking of."

As we pull up in front of a row of little trailer homes, a man in a wool coat opens the door to a blue one, his collar pulled up high. He looks around nervously, then books it full speed to his car. *Don't worry, bud. No one here is judging you for anything other than those ugly sneakers.* Tabitha gets out and starts toward that blue trailer without saying anything. *Okay then.* I follow her.

The door opens before she can knock.

"Tabby! Baby! I missed you so much!" A familiar-looking woman practically jumps out of the trailer, her arms spread wide. *Sorry, lady, Tabby isn't gonna come in for a hug if that's what you're waiting for.* "Look at you! You look so good! My goodness!"

Tabitha scoffs, stopping a couple of feet in front of the lady. *Hmm.* Why does she look so familiar? It's the hairstyle for sure. Short, sleek, and black, like a nineteen-twenties flapper, with a sparkly headband of gold coins around it. The lady drops her arms, stuffs her hands into the pockets of her flowing, yellow silk robe, and shivers.

"My goodness, it's cold out. Let's get inside so you can tell me all about what's going on." Finally, she acknowledges me with a smile and a wave toward the open door. "You too, now. Any friend of Tabby's is a friend of mine. Oh, and you're lucky because Angela's here tonight. She made that cake you like, Tabby."

Angela. Then, it clicks. This is *Klaire Voyant*, and she has to be referring to *Angelust.* I'm about to go sit in a room with the three hottest female Villains to ever form a trio. *Holy shit.*

Back when Tabitha was Poison Princess, she teamed up with Klaire and Angela. I remember times when I'd turn on the news and see Tabitha break down a door, stomp inside in her skimpy outfit, and right behind her were those two hot as hell chicks ready to help kick ass. Damn, those clips got played on repeat many, many times.

"Are you coming, you slow ass?" Tabitha drawls.

"Oh, sorry." I snap out of the staring thing and scurry into the trailer.

It's a lot nicer inside than I thought it would be. Like, really nice. Everything is super clean, and all the items look thoughtfully chosen and placed. It's spacious, tidy, and homey. The whole place smells like yellow cake and contains a surprising number of ceramic cats.

"Why don't you come back to my room. If we're doing some deep memory work, it'll be the comfiest," Klaire says as she opens a door at the far end of the trailer. She stops before entering to smile at me. "I'm Klaire, by the way. Should introduce myself before I go digging through your mind."

"Wait, what?" I look at Tabitha for an explanation, but she's already halfway into Klaire's room. I speak up so they can hear me. "What do you mean by digging through my mind?"

A door across from me opens, and a tiny, cherub-cheeked woman with soaking wet, cherry-red hair looks at me with surprise.

"Oh, hey there! I'm sorry, hon. Are you here for me or Klaire? If you're here for me, I gotta apologize for my lack of preparation. I wasn't expecting an appointment so soon," she says, patting her face and hair nervously. "Oh my goodness, I don't even have lipstick on."

"You're fine, no. You look great." I give her a thumbs-up that seems to calm her down a bit. "I'm here with Tabitha. To see Klaire, I guess. Uh, I'm supposed to go in there now, actually. I don't really know what's going on."

"Tabby's here? Oh good! I'll have to get decent and come see y'all. I'm Angela, hon. Pleasure meeting you." She holds out her hand. Without thinking, I shake it.

"I'm Henry, nice to...meet...you." My words are slow, and my mind relaxes. I feel like I'm not even sure if I'm awake anymore. *Am I awake?*

"A real pleasure, Henry," Angela says with a grin as she walks her fingers slowly up my arm. She giggles when she reaches my shoulder. "You seem so sweet. I could do very, very bad things to you. I think you'd like them very, very much."

Her voice floats past like a satin scarf brushing smoothly along my cheek and then disappearing. The ceramic cats wink at me and flash their pink tongues. Angela's little fingers dance and kick on my shoulder at full speed while everything else is so slow and thick. Like yellow cake batter. I know if she wants to, she could change this. She could do those very bad things she mentioned. And I *know* I would like them. She's Ange*lust* for a reason.

"Leave him alone, I'm trying to see if he's a jerk or not," Tabitha barks, her voice clear even in the muck.

"Oh, fine." Angela stops touching me, and shortly after, things start to clear up. "Shoo, before I change my mind."

As much as I would like to see what her legendary pleasure touch could do, that's not what I'm here for. I'm a Tabby man.

In Klaire's room, I find a grumpy-looking Tabitha sitting on a plastic folding chair, Klaire sitting cross-legged on a large, purple cushion, and a second folding chair between them.

Klaire pats the empty chair, then straightens her posture. "Come on, buddy boy. Sit down. Let me get into those brains."

I do not sit down.

"Nope. This is weird. I did not consent to this. What the hell is going on?"

Tabitha rolls her eyes at me. "Stop being dramatic. I just have to make sure you're not gonna betray me or something."

"I'm not!"

"But I don't know that! This way I can make an educated decision."

"That's not how dating or any kind of relationship works. You have to take risks, get to know each other, learn to trust—"

"I already told her that," Klaire says.

Tabitha scoffs. "Yeah, that's stupid. *Trust* got me into so much trouble. I'm over it."

"Let's get this over with, then. Come on, Henry. Just spill all your smelly old beans." Klaire pats the chair again.

They sound kind of convincing. I mean, I don't have bad intentions, and I'm not planning on hurting Tabitha.

Ugh, I can't believe I'm going to do this.

"Alright, but don't mess up my brain. It's the only one I have," I say as I sit down next to Klaire.

"Scouts honor," Tabitha says drily.

"I very highly doubt you were a scout."

"Hey, you don't know what I did before they frog-fucked my DNA," she says indignantly. After a moment of silence during which Klaire adjusts our positions, I hear Tabitha say under her breath, "Definitely was not a scout, though."

"Okay, kiddo. I'm going to surf rapidly through your memories. It might tickle, but it shouldn't take *too* long. Tabitha would like to know when you became interested in the Blessed, and whether your interest is a danger to her. The answers aren't always straightforward, but I'll share what feels right. Henry, I'm assuming you've seen how that works?" Klaire asks in a professional tone, as if this is a therapy appointment or something, rather than an intrusion on the entirety of my memory.

"Yeah, I've seen it." *In a documentary on why she was sent to prison, for fuck's sake.*

"Okay! Well, close your eyes, relax, and let's go!"

When she takes my hand, the feeling is immediate and intense. Every moment of my life crashes against the back of my eyelids. It's all moving so fast that it becomes a blur of colors, but I know what's happening, and I feel it all the same.

I do not like this. Not one bit.

My jaw clenches, then all the muscles in the rest of my body tighten, trying to fight against the horrible internal intrusion. A whine breaks free from my throat. Every feeling, every emotion, I've ever had slams into me at warp speed. I *really* do not like this.

"Ssh. Getting closer," Klaire says, her voice deep, sensual.

It lasts only a few seconds longer—though even that moment feels like ages—before everything stills. This is it. This is her showstopper.

She found something.

"Open your eyes, Henry. Tell us what's happening."

We're no longer in the trailer. At least, for the moment, it doesn't look that way. The three of us are in my memory. It's not a good one.

"Holy shit, is that you?" Tabitha asks.

Klaire shushes her. "Tabitha, quiet. Let Henry guide us."

I can see why Tabitha is shocked. The young man on the table barely looks like me.

"Yeah. That's me. First year of teaching." I feel tears well up in the corners of my eyes. "Took a few sick days that first year."

Younger Henry has his shirt off as the doctor inspects him—me. All of the signs of my illness are on display. He presses the stethoscope against my bony chest and frowns when I take a shaky breath. He asks if I've been eating. I say I have, but that's a lie. My hollow stomach and visible ribs tell the truth. He asks me to show him why I'm there. I tell him I'm a teacher, and I got a scratch from a kid, and now it's gotten really bad. I twist my arm and show him the underside, where a tiny fingernail grazed me at the start of the year. The doctor flinches at the sight of it, so I know I'm right—it's bad. He says the wound on my arm is turning septic and that he wants to run a few tests. He thinks something else is wrong, too. He prescribes medicine for my arm before I go to the lab.

The room fades out and back in again. The same doctor's office, another day. I find out that I'm very, very sick, and that it can't be fixed. At least my arm is getting better.

A different room now. I'm sitting in front of my students—standing for too long was hard those days—while a presenter from the wildlife rehab center hands me an opossum. The little kids shriek and giggle at the sight of the strange animal.

Then it's only a moment later, and half of my students are gone, and I'm screaming for help. A school bus crashes into the side of the building.

The room fades out and into that doctor's office again. This time I'm looking much more like myself, though still thinner than I should be. The doctor inspects my opossum tail. I tell him that I've felt better since the Mash-Up. He takes a blood sample. There's a flash forward, and when he returns, he's laughing with delight as he tells me I'm no longer sick.

Whatever happened to me in the Mash-Up saved my life.

Fade out and in again, but now we're in my apartment. I'm online, trying to find out if anything like that had happened to anyone else. Turns out, it had. There are whole forums devoted to discussing it. I click on one and find a picture of Poison Princess caught in a provocative pose mid-fight. There's an article attached talking about how she found a serial killer and fucked him up. It gets me looking further into this supposed Villain, and I end up finding tons of incidents of her being more vigilante than Villain. There are a lot of pictures in the articles.

My apartment fades away, and I'm back in Klaire's room.

"So, yeah. My interest in Poison Princess turned into a thing for gifted people in general. I just think powers are really fucking cool, which I think is understandable considering I would have died had Darkiss not used his. And to be honest, I'm a kinky little freak anyway. It might have happened whether I was sick or not. I don't know what else to say." I wrap my arms around my knees and glare at Tabitha. "Can we stay out of my head now?"

Tabitha nods. "Yeah."

Klaire claps, then rubs her hands together. "Your turn, Tabby."

Tabitha snorts. "Yeah, right. Very funny."

Klaire's smile disappears. "Put your hand in hers, Henry. I'll have to work through you. This'll be fun. I've never been able to do Tabby before."

Tabitha looks for an exit. Unfortunately for her, she's blocked in.

"Fair's fair, Tabitha." Klaire taps a long, red fingernail against her tooth while she thinks. "Oh! Let Henry ask a question, and we'll dig up the answer. That's what you did."

"This is bullshit," Tabitha growls.

"No, Klaire's right. It is fair. We do this now, and then after that, never again. But I do have a question I think you should answer." As I approach Tabitha, she shrinks away from me, steps backwards until she's against the wall. When there's nowhere else for her to go, I take her hand, look into the endlessness of her eyes, and ask, "Are you going to hurt me?"

Chapter Eleven

Tabitha

As soon as Klaire touches Henry, everything goes to shit. She's in my head. I can feel her digging around. It's so gross. Ugh. Just when I think I can't handle it anymore, she makes a satisfied sound, and the room changes.

"Oh, fuck," I mumble.

We all look to the side and watch the show—my past—play out in glorious color. We're in for a fucked-up evening.

We're in a small apartment with yellow floral curtains on the window.

"Not my mother," I snap. "Move on, Klaire."

Thankfully, she hears the seriousness in my voice. The woman disappears.

A new room fades in. A young girl with dyed black hair stands at a desk with two adults, signing papers. There's something off about the adults—as if their smiles are painted on—but the girl and the ones giving her away are joyful, unaware of the danger. As soon as they leave, and the adults get the girl into their car, their smiles drop. False as paint all along.

"They had a deal. They could take the trouble-makers. No chance anyone would snoop around then because no one wanted kids like us."

My knees buckle when the next room shows up. The bright light overhead. My body strapped to a cold table. The needles aimed directly at my eyes. They were still a light shade of brown then.

"No. Stop. Klaire, STOP!" I hold my hands in front of Henry's face. I don't want him, or anyone, to see this.

"I'm sorry," Klaire says as the scene shifts, "I'm so sorry, Tabby."

My heart is still racing as the room fades into the next memory. I'm me as I am now. The experiments have been done. They'd put me in a straitjacket and slapped a mask over the lower part of my face. I have a black eye from daring to tell a guard I wasn't hungry one day. In fact, I have a lot of bruises.

"I was only fifteen," I say quietly, mostly to myself at this point. "Just a kid. I'd already been there for years, though. Every day was hell."

Then the room shakes. I perk up. Everything rocks and shudders as if there's an earthquake. I look around for somewhere to hide from the falling tiles, but everything's been taken from my room already. I growl in frustration right before the door flies open. The guard who blackened my eye soars into and across the room, slamming into the wall behind me with a bone-shattering crunch.

I mumble, "Fuck you, then," to his corpse and book it out the door. On the other side of it is—

"Darkiss!" Henry says, voice dripping with awe. I understand it.

His presence commands respect. I waddled out there with my hair in tangles, half-starved and beaten. He called for all the prisoners to escape or follow him. It was our choice. He spoke directly to a few of us, however—Angela, Bradley, Klaire, and me.

He said, "Come with me, children. Stay by my side, and I promise you'll be safe. I swear you'll have revenge on those who have harmed you."

It took no thought at all to follow him.

"We *were* all children, too. That's the saddest thing. I don't know if that's why he chose us, or maybe we were just the angriest of the bunch. Either way, he asked, and we followed. A few others did as well, but none of them stayed around for long. Just the four of us."

Fade out to a tiny prison cell in the Villain rehabilitation ward. I cry when I see that the food on my tray has been tampered with again. The only light I have goes off, leaving me alone in the dark.

I feel numb. She didn't even show the worst bits of my life, not even close, yet Henry is looking at me like I'm the most pathetically sad creature that has ever existed.

"I wasn't born wanting to hurt people, Henry—but I'm not ashamed of the times I did. I was a soft, little girl for a very short time. The world made me a monster."

"You're not a monster, Tabitha," Henry says in an admirable attempt to soothe me.

"No, I am. And the people who made me got what they deserved for being so stupid. They thought they could create something so much better, stronger, and vicious than them, *torture* her, then live to tell the tale?" I scoff. "I'm not *worse* for being a monster. I only regret having to live among such fragile beings."

The room is so silent I can hear my own heartbeat. It's then that I realize that, perhaps, I've said too much. Maybe even said things I hadn't admitted to myself before. Well, what's done is done.

"It's up to you whether you think you can trust me or not. I won't hurt you if you don't hurt me. I think that's what Klaire's selection of greatest hits was trying to show. Personally, I think I'm perfectly stable now. Just had a rough few years."

It's Henry's turn to scoff. "A rough few years? That's what you're calling it?"

I shrug.

"Well, I think we're done, Klaire," Henry says.

"Alrighty!" Klaire shakes out her hands. "That was a great session, you guys."

As soon as Henry stops touching me, I slip my arm into my sleeve, make a fist inside it, march over to Klaire, and punch her in the arm.

"Ow! What was that for?" she whines.

"Oh, I don't know: showing me being tortured, my mom, Darkiss, et cetera. You're such a butthole." I punch her again for good measure.

"Oh, whatever. You're fine!" She waves dismissively. "Besides, I can already feel how much closer it brought you two together. Everyone needs some trauma dumping sometimes, you know?"

"No! Some people are fine keeping things bottled up."

She sticks her tongue out at me. I squint at her. Henry laughs.

"You two are great," he says.

I look at him with an eyebrow raised. "You're already over this traumatic shitshow?"

He shrugs.

"Fine. We're all crazy. Just fucking nuts." I sigh.

"You didn't need me to help you figure that out." Klaire gives Henry and me the once over. "You two give off whacko vibes like no one else."

I pull my hood up. "It was lovely seeing you, Klaire. Have a good night."

She laughs and wraps her arms around Henry in a friendly hug. "Goodnight, you two. Visit any time. I won't dig around in your heads if you don't want me to."

"I definitely will *not* want that," Henry says.

On the way out the door, Klaire stops Henry. "Bring your brother around next time. From what I saw in your memories, I think he and Angela would get along nicely."

As soon as he and I are on the road, Henry says, "Okay, what the hell was that about Mark and Angela?"

The absolute confusion on his face has me cracking up laughing out loud. Life with Klaire was like that. She'd drop unexpected things on us all the time.

"If I were you, I would pass that message on to Mark. Klaire's intuition is pretty good. I mean, she's kind of known for it."

"Oh, really? I didn't know." Henry laughs. "I don't know how Mark will react to that news. He shares custody with his ex. He might not want to date a former Villain who works as a—"

"Don't judge her. He's not better than her because he's a lawyer."

"What? No! I'm not judging her, I swear. The family courts can just be really shitty sometimes, and his ex-wife is really vindictive. She'd use anything she could to take Jimmy." Henry glances at me, still trying to keep his focus on the road, but it's long enough that I can see he's sincere. "Alright?"

"Yeah. Okay."

We drive through the dark streets in silence a little longer before I see something that makes me break it. I point ahead of us to an empty lot on the otherwise occupied street.

"Pull over."

Henry looks at me curiously but does as I ask. The street's dead this time of night, so there's no one to bother us as we sit here parked. This spot has been empty for the last decade. It makes a hollow between the other buildings that reminds me of a missing tooth. When I don't immediately speak up, Henry clears his throat and does it for me.

"This is the first place you made your public appearance as Poison Princess."

I turn to him and look him up and down in appraisal. "Well, someone's done their homework."

"Yes, ma'am. I'm sure to be a straight-A student."

Sudden thoughts of bending him over and spanking him with a ruler flash before my eyes. *Where the fuck did that come from?* I turn away before he can see me blush.

"Yeah, this was the Park Optometry Clinic, an undercover outpost of the institute. The first place we went once the crew was trained. Our first target for revenge. His name was Doctor Chase," I say.

I let the memories flood back, reliving the scene as I tell the story to Henry.

"Stonecrash—Bradley—blew the whole front of the building open. Klaire scanned the place for anyone involved with experimenting on us. Angela got all the innocent people out of the way—though admittedly, she toyed with them. She wasn't the most mentally stable at the time and tended to lash out at bystanders. None of us were stable, to be fair, but I couldn't risk using my ability on anyone who didn't absolutely deserve punishment. When we found scientists we recognized, I touched them. Quickly killed the ones less *directly* involved in our torture. But Doctor Chase?" I smile and rest my cheek against the cool glass of the car window, letting myself remember the look on his face as he screamed. "First, Angela commanded him to lie still so we could tie him down. Then, Klaire got into his head. Made him feel the things they did to us. Finally, I barely, just *barely*, grazed him with the tip of my finger. Let the poison *burn* through him slowly. Get to his brain. Because, Henry, if the poison doesn't kill someone, it *keeps* burning. Not only that, there are hallucinations. Horrible ones. There's no way to stop them either. Pain and terror. Forever."

"From what I remember reading, you left Doctor Chase alive in the rubble," Henry says softly. "When the emergency services arrived, everyone else was gone or dead, but he was strapped to an exam chair, screaming. The rest of the building had crumbled around him."

"That's true. Stonecrash made sure he wasn't crushed when we brought it down."

"Is Doctor Chase still alive? If there's no antidote to your poison, then that means he's been like that this whole time."

"As far as I know, yes." Thankfully, my body is blocking the reflection of my smile from Henry.

"Holy shit."

"Hopefully, you understand why it's important that no one knows you can touch me. Klaire and Angela are fine. They're like family. And, obviously, Mark. No one beyond that can know. There are people who will do anything to find an antidote." Now I look at Henry. "Doctor Chase has a wife, for example. A scientist as well, though she didn't work at Geiger Falls when I was there. I don't know where she is now, but if she's anything like her husband, I'm sure she'd do anything to get her hands on a potential cure like you. I don't think she'd treat you kindly should they get a hold of you either."

Henry's throat bobs as he swallows, his eyes wide with fear. He turns toward the front, puts his hands on the steering wheel, and nods. After letting out a shaky breath, he speaks again.

"Why is it you're always either saying almost nothing or the most fucked up shit?" He rests his head on the top of the steering wheel and turns to look at me when I bark out a surprised laugh. "You're scary and weird. I like it though. I like you. A lot."

There's no time to turn away before the blush flames hot in my cheeks. Hopefully, the dark of the evening hides it. I nervously inspect my gloved hands as he continues talking.

"I promise I won't let anyone know about the touch thing. Let's do whatever we need to do so that neither of us ends up in a jail cell or as a science experiment. Alright?"

"Okay."

"And then we can maybe see each other? And do some of that touching, possibly? Sound good?"

I lift my head to look at him and find him sitting straight now, smiling at me.

"Just drive."

"I'm taking that as a yes."

"Start the car and take a right, is what you mean. It's bedtime."

"Is that an invitation? Or?"

I glare at him.

"You are *very* lucky you're immune to me."

He grins widely as he starts the car. "Yeah, I am."

On the short drive home, we talk a little about work, nothing too serious. I admit I'm a bit sad when we pull up to my apartment. I hesitate when I reach for the handle of the car door, wondering whether I should invite him up, but I decide against it. I don't want to give him the wrong idea. I do, however, allow him to walk me to my apartment door. The hallway is dark, and at this time of night, no one is around to attempt small talk.

Henry walks me all the way to my inside door. I fit my key into the lock and turn back to him for our goodnight.

"Well, despite all the messed-up parts, I'm glad we had this night together, Henry."

"Me too. A little mess every once in a while won't kill anyone."

"Well—"

"Shush, you. Always with the gloom and doom."

"I can't believe you shushed me."

Henry raises an eyebrow. "Are you pouting?"

"No!" I'm lying to myself and to him.

"You're pouting. And it's *cute.*"

"It's not cute because I'm not pouting!"

Henry pushes my hood back and tucks my hair behind my ears.

"Let me get a better look," he says playfully.

Any bit of the previous emotion is gone by the time he runs his thumb along my jaw. I'm certainly not pouting. Not sure I'm even breathing.

"Looks like I was wrong," he says quietly as he leans toward me, his eyelids drifting closed.

Shit. He's going to kiss me. I think? What do I do?

My brain finally screams something smart at me for once.

KISS HIM BACK!

I, perhaps a bit too forcefully, smash my face against his. To his credit, he doesn't let my awkwardness ruin the mood. Instead, Henry works his fingers through my hair and gently guides me through my first grown-up kiss. It's soft, and a tiny bit clumsy, but *Oh My God* is it great. When Henry pulls away, his eyes look totally different. I've never seen an expression like that in them. It's like he—oh. *Oh.* He wants to have sex. Those are *ready for sex* eyes. I take a step back and grab the door handle.

"That was...Wow," I say, breathlessly.

Henry strokes my cheek, that same hungry look still flaring bright.

"Wow, is right."

"I should go now."

"Are you sure?"

"Yep." I turn the handle and crack the door open, slipping inside. I stick my arm out and wave right before closing it. "Bye!"

I run to the bathroom, splash water on my face, and wipe it dry. I look up into the mirror above the sink and, even through the pure blackness, I can see the same hungry expression in my eyes that I just saw in Henry's.

I want more.

Chapter Twelve

Henry

Despite giving me a bloody lip and then being really weird afterward, that was the most amazing kiss ever. I had to sit in my car and recover for a few minutes before driving home because I knew my mind would be way too occupied with her to focus on the road. Dickstracted driving is dangerous.

When I finally got home, settled in, and tried to sleep, I failed epically. No matter how much I tried to relax and clear my mind, all my thoughts returned to her.

By the time the phone rings in the morning, I've only managed to scrape together maybe two hours of shut-eye. With the gravel of sleep still in my voice, I answer, "Hidey-ho!"

"You sound like shit," Mark says, far too chipper for my liking. "How was last night?"

I take my time to reply, rubbing my eyes and loudly yawning. When I'm sure he's annoyed, I answer, "I think it was *almost* a date."

"Whoa! Hold on! That's big news. Are you seeing her now?"

A smile takes over my face that I don't think is going to leave any time soon. "Yeah. I think so, anyway. She's confusing."

Mark laughs. "The best women are."

I stand up and stretch, then head toward the kitchen. Time for coffee.

"You know, her friend wants to hook you up with someone."

"How does her friend know about me?"

"Eh, it's complicated. I guess her judgment is pretty good. The girl is cute. She bakes. Maybe you should check her out. I know you haven't been on a date in a while."

"A while? It's been so long since I've gotten laid, I'm pretty sure I've got dust in my balls. I'd just shoot cobwebs out of my dick. Like a really sad, lonely Spider-Man."

"That's tragic, brother. You should go out with her. Though there is a small conflict—potential one anyway—but she's really nice."

I start the coffee maker and sit at the kitchen counter to wait.

"Potential conflict? That doesn't sound great, Henry."

"Well, she's a former Villain."

Mark sighs.

"And her current profession isn't *exactly* legal."

"Okay. So maybe not the best choice for the lawyer-slash-father with the litigious, vindictive ex?"

His ex-wife, Janine, really will use *any* trick in the book to hurt him legally. I feel for him.

"She's *really* pretty." I can't help laughing when he scoffs. "And you love redheads. Come on. Let's go on a double date. It'll be fun."

"Henry. You didn't say she was a *redhead*."

Got him. Now to hit him in the fetish.

"She has a southern accent, too. It's real thick."

Mark groans in frustration. I don't know what it is, but he loves a thick southern accent on a woman. He's a total sucker for it. Combine that with a sweet redhead who can bake? I think Klaire is on to something.

After a pause, he says, "A double date?"

"Yep. No one on the outside has to know anything is happening. If Janine snoops around, it'll look like we're all just hanging out. If you like her, then you can decide if you want to take the chance and date her, ex be damned. If you don't like her, then no harm was done." The coffee pot sputters as the water slows. Almost done. "How does that sound?"

He takes a minute to respond, but when he does, he sounds...hopeful? Which is great, considering I haven't heard that from him when it comes to women in a long time.

"Fine. Just let me know the details. What's her name? I suppose I should know that."

"It's Angela." I grab my cup and pour some coffee. "What did you call about, by the way?"

"Oh, yeah, that's important. Can you watch the little guy this afternoon? I know it's last-minute, but I have some big news with a client, and it would be good to get to it as soon as possible."

"Sure. Send him over." I dump some sugar in my coffee and stir it around. "We'll watch cartoons."

"Okay, great. Thanks! See you later!"

I'm about to hang up when Mark says something else.

"Hey, wait. You don't mean Angela as in *Angelust?* Like Tabitha's... associate? The one with the sex powers?"

I almost spit out my coffee.

"That's her. Talk to you later." I hang up before he can say anything else.

Once I make myself comfortable on the sofa, I open my contacts to call the gorgeous, grumpy goddess whose scowling face I can't stop daydreaming about. I take a deep breath and then...chicken out and toss my phone onto the cushion next to me. Then, I take another sip of coffee, ruffle my hair, shake out my arms, and take another breath. Now I'm ready for another shot. I stare at her contact information, sweat beading on my forehead, before finally hitting the call button. My stomach rumbles as it rings, waves of coffee and sugar swishing around in my gut as I wait for her answer. After several rings, she picks up.

"What?" She sounds predictably grouchy, with a tinge of sleepiness.

"Hi! It's me, Henry."

"I know. Phones have caller ID."

"Oh, yeah." I clear my throat. "So, I was thinking about how Klaire said that Angela would be a good match for Mark."

"Okay."

"What if we went on a double date?" There's silence on the other end for long enough that I'm not sure whether or not she's still there, so I ask to make sure. "Tabitha? You there?"

"Yeah."

"Did you hear what I said?"

"Yeah." Another pause, then she finally says, "I've never been asked on a date before. I don't know. Don't say anything weird."

Oh, wow. Okay.

"Well, that's a shame. We can go wherever you want to then. Or I can pick. Your choice."

"Um, not every place is welcoming to people like Angela and me, so it's probably best if she and I pick the place."

"Oh shit, I didn't think of that. I'm sorry, people suck."

"Yeah."

"What day works best for you?"

"Any early evening or weekend. Same as you. You know my work schedule."

I laugh. "Yeah, true. What about Angela?"

"She doesn't exactly have a schedule. I mean, she gets bookings, but if she has to reschedule with someone, she will."

"Oh, that's cool. I've always wanted a job where I decide my own hours."

"I'm sure she could help you get into her industry."

"I doubt there would be enough demand for someone like me—"

"Oh, come on. Mashies? Huge market. Major demand. Especially handsome, slender, tall, bisexual ones? You'd have a line out the door."

I'm glad no one is around to see how hard I'm blushing right now. Also, how hard something else is getting.

"Tabitha, I don't think that's for me, but if you'd like to continue to tell me how attractive I am, please do so."

She laughs, a full, hearty one. The sound is a rare delight, and my heart skips a beat when I hear it.

"Where do you live? Angela and I can pick a place in your area and meet you there. Sooner the better, because I hate waiting. How about tomorrow evening? Six."

"I hate waiting too, so that's good for me—assuming Mark is fine with it. I can pick you up, so you don't have to meet us."

"Angela will want to meet up. I know her."

"If you insist."

I give her my address, we say our goodbyes, and afterwards I text Mark. Though he's surprised we scheduled it so soon, he says he's okay with it. Everything is settled. A couple of hours after that, he arrives with my nephew in tow.

The tiny, cherub-cheeked boy leaps into my arms as soon as the door opens. I lift him over my head and wiggle him around until he laughs.

"Hey there, Jimmy-Jam. You ready to have some fun?"

"Yeah!"

"I wish I could stay and have fun with you, too. Unfortunately, duty calls. I'll be back before sunset." Mark plants a loud smooch on Jimmy's cheek that has him shrieking with laughter. "Be good for Henry, Jim-Jam."

"Bye-bye, Daddy!"

The next couple of hours are smooth sailing. He's a good kid, doesn't make much of a fuss. By the end of the afternoon, we're both lazing on my sofa, eating chips, watching cartoons, and just vibing. It's nice and quiet. Then, my phone buzzes. I check the screen, thinking it must be Mark, but to my surprise, it's Tabitha. My stomach sinks. *I hope she's not canceling our date.* I hit the green button to answer.

"Hey, Tabitha. What's up?"

"I'm outside."

"What? Outside where?"

"Outside of your building."

What the hell? "I'm just letting you know that sounds creepy."

Jimmy pulls a damp potato chip out of his mouth and looks at me with big eyes. "Uncle Henny! Did you say creeper? There's a game! My cousin, he has a game on his phone, and there are scary guys, and—" Jimmy grabs my face with his chubby hands to make sure I'm listening to him, "on the phone! There are scary creepers on the game, Uncle Henny!"

I nod along, even though I have no idea what game he's talking about, and when he's done, I add a thoughtful, "Wow, goodness."

Jimmy returns my nod, shoves the wet chip back into his mouth, and turns back toward the television.

"Who was that?" Tabitha asks.

"My nephew. I'm babysitting."

"Oh. Never mind. I was going to come say hi for a minute, but I'll—"

"No, no! Come on up!" I hop off the sofa and slide over to the front door buzzer. "Let me buzz you in."

"I don't think it's a good idea. I shouldn't be around little—"

"Come on, just for a minute."

She sighs just before I hear footsteps on stairs in the background.

"Okay, but you have to keep the kid away, don't forget. Seriously."

"I promise! Obviously!"

Bzz! I hit the button to let her in, excitedly bouncing on my toes, waiting for her. *This is so awesome.* Tabitha. In my apartment. *Ah!* Two solid knocks on the cheap wood, I unlock the door, then there she is.

"Who's there?" Jimmy shouts as he springs to his feet on the sofa cushions.

"It's my friend, Tabitha." I step away from the door and gesture for her to enter. She peers around the room warily from under her hood for a moment before finally slinking inside. "She's just saying hi."

"Hi," she mumbles.

"Hi Patiba!" Jimmy says with full confidence as he holds onto the back of the sofa, jumping up and down. "Do you like cartoons?"

"I don't know," she says as she crosses her arms.

"You never watched 'em?" Jimmy asks, shoving another chip into his mouth as he curiously inspects Tabitha.

"Not really." She swings a plastic bag in her hand as she rocks back and forth in her tall boots. "Didn't have a TV when I was a kid."

Jimmy's mouth drops open, and his bouncing ceases.

"No T.V.? Patiba! Come here! Sit down!"

"Uh, Tabitha is going to stay on that side of the room, Jimmy. She has a cold and doesn't want to get you sick. Okay, buddy? Let's all just stay separated." I ruffle his hair and scoot him down into a sitting position. "Let me go talk to Tabitha for a minute."

"Aww, fine," Jimmy whines.

Tabitha huffs a laugh as I approach her.

"Don't come too close. I don't want to get you sick," she says quietly.

"I'll take the chance." I nod in the direction of the hall, and we walk so that we're far enough away from the kid where I can see him, but he can't hear us. "So, why are you here? Just decided to stalk me?"

"Pfft. I was getting groceries." She pulls an orange out of the bag and holds it up as proof. "The store by my place has *kindly* asked that I not shop there anymore. Now I have to come all the way over here. I figured since I was so close, I'd say hi. Maybe that's weird. I don't know. I'm not good at this."

I laugh as I take hold of her hand, the one not holding an orange, and twine my fingers together with hers.

"Hey, no one ever really knows what they're doing. The point is to just do it."

"Well, then, I did it."

"Yes, you did."

And then, *Bzz!*

My stomach drops.

"Another friend?" Jimmy yells.

"No, bud." I look at a concerned Tabitha and swallow the dread sticking in my throat. "It's your dad."

"Yay!" he shouts as he jumps off the couch and races to slap the door buzzer.

"Is this going to be a problem?" Tabitha asks. "Because if it is, you shouldn't have let me come up here."

"Um, it should—I mean, I think it will be fine because Mark—"

Jimmy unlocks the door as soon as he can make out the sound of footsteps in the hall. The door swings open, and Mark scoops him up in his arms.

"Argh, I missed you, Jim-Jam! Did you have fun?"

"Yeah! I met Patiba, but she's sick, so don't go over there, okay? She doesn't have a TV. Can she come watch at my house?"

Mark looks around, confused, before seeing the dark figure standing halfway down the side hallway. His face changes from cheerfully curious to angry and protective in an instant. He sets Jimmy down and steps in front of him.

"Hey, Jim, get your shoes on, then come right back to me. Don't touch anything else."

Tabitha scoffs. As Jimmy retrieves his shoes, Mark glances at me out of the side of his eye.

"What the *fuck* are you thinking, Henry?"

"He's fine, Mark."

"One touch." Mark's voice shakes as Jimmy returns to him. "One touch and he'd be—you know what."

"I wouldn't hurt him. I've never hurt a kid, Mark," Tabitha says.

"I don't believe you would do it *intentionally*. I really, truly believe that. But accidents happen."

The two of them lock eyes, and Tabitha wraps her arms tightly around herself again.

"Yeah. Sorry, Mark," she says. Then, much softer, again, "Sorry."

Mark picks up Jimmy and sighs, his face relaxing. "No harm done, Tabitha."

She nods, her gaze to her feet.

"Hey, you like oranges, Patiba?" Jimmy pipes up.

Everyone, including Tabitha, looks at him and finds that he's looking at her. She holds up the orange still clutched in her hand.

"Yeah, I do."

"I like 'em cuz my mom says they'll make me strong." Jimmy flexes his little arms before wrapping them around Mark's neck.

"Oh, uh, I like them because they have a thick, protective outer layer, and I can divide them into even pieces." She shifts awkwardly from foot to foot. "I like it when my food is even."

"You're silly," Jimmy says. "Are you gonna have babies with Henry?"

"Okay, time to go," Mark says, quickly turning toward the door. "I'll see you tomorrow, Tabitha."

"Oh, okay, good," Tabitha says, surprise evident in her reply. I admit, I'm surprised he still wants to go too.

After I shut the door behind them, I turn to Tabitha with my hands folded together. My tail wraps around her thigh and squeezes.

"Please don't be mad. I'm sorry, seriously. That was awkward as fuck, I know."

She slaps me on the arm with her bag of oranges. "There. You get grocery-smacked because I was right that I shouldn't have come up here."

"Wow, okay. Cruel and unusual punishment, but I guess I'll take whatever you give me."

She sighs and rubs my arm. "Well, you were also pretty sweet."

I lean back against the door and smirk.

"Yeah?"

"Mhm. And, I admit, you look exceptionally good in those pants."

"These pants? Um, they're just sweatpants."

Tabitha steps close enough for her breasts to press against me. Her bag of groceries hits the floor with a *thump.* She looks into my eyes as she runs her hands down my sides, from my waist all the way down my hips, then up the fronts of my thighs.

"I like them a lot," she says softly, her lips nearly grazing mine. "I liked our kiss yesterday, too. I couldn't stop thinking about it. Will you kiss me again, Henry?"

My lips press against hers, *fuck yes is* the answer they give. The only answer I can ever imagine giving her.

This kiss is much different from our first. The full weight of her is pressed against me, flattening me to the door. Her hands are on either side of my head, her feet planted on the outsides of mine. I'm pinned in place. She kisses hard and hungrily, as if she's claiming me. I think if she were given the option, she'd eat my face.

I feel a little scared, to be honest.

I fucking *love* it.

After she's violated my mouth for several minutes, she pulls back, glances down between us, and tilts her head. She steps back, licks her lips, and smirks with an eyebrow raised. I wait for her to give me the news, whatever it may be.

"You're hard, Henry," she says.

I can't help but laugh.

"Yeah, very much so. You just tongue-fucked my mouth, so, uh, not surprising."

She stands with her hands on my shoulders, looking at the outline of my erection appraisingly. I've never felt so self-conscious in my life. She bites her bottom lip and runs her hands along my biceps.

"I've never touched one before. Would it be wrong if I touched you? We only first kissed yesterday, so if I'm moving too fast for you, say something. I just really want to know what you feel like," she says as she trails a finger down my stomach.

My mouth has gone dry as fuck, so it takes a second before I can unstick my tongue from the roof of my mouth to reply.

"I think you should do what you're comfortable with. As fast or slow as you want to go is fine with me." *But fuck if I'm not wishing for fast.*

She bites her lip again as she runs her hands along my waistband, the velvet softness of her gloves tickling the bare skin of my stomach with each pass. Her choice becomes clear when she places her hands flat against my abs and smiles. My breathing quickens—the sparkle in the blackness of her eyes tells me this is going to be *so fucking good*.

"I need to take off these gloves," she says.

"Oh, of course," I reply, voice wavering like a virgin.

The twenty or so seconds it takes her to remove those black gloves are the longest seconds of my life. She tugs them off one finger at a time, and each one makes me want to scream "Hurry!" but I'm patient. When she's done, I'm aching for her to touch me.

"Can I pull these down?" she asks.

"Do whatever the fuck you want," I answer breathlessly.

She undoes the drawstring in what feels like slow motion before jerking my pants and boxers both down below my hips. My cock is already leaking as it bounces out of its fabric prison. I think it's a decently impressive specimen, but I'm not sure what exactly Tabitha is into, if she even has a preference.

"I'm just going to feel you. Don't expect anything exciting. I don't know what I'm doing," she says, a blush appearing on her cheeks as she shyly tucks her chin into her shoulder.

"Don't get shy all of a sudden, Tabitha. It's alright. I'm not expecting anything. Whatever you do is good."

"Okay." She locks eyes with me, the awkwardness fading, a mix of curiosity and desire replacing it. I keep my eyes on hers as her warm, moist fingertips tentatively graze my shaft. "Oh, it's so soft. The skin, I mean. I didn't expect it to feel like that."

I nod, keeping our gaze connected. Tabitha lightly touches the head of my cock, and I can't help the desperate breath that escapes me. She tips her head to the side, then wraps her hand around my throbbing dick just below the crown, gently squeezing, before slowly pumping up and down in short, focused strokes. My hips buck at the unexpected action.

"Fuck, Tabitha. That's just how I like it."

"Is it? Good." She steps back, leans down, and spits on my cock, before increasing the speed of her hand. "I read about what to do. Just never thought I'd do it."

My eyes roll back momentarily, and I have to force them forward again. She's grinning when I look back at her. My muscles tighten up, and my tail must be cutting off the blood supply to her thigh by now, so I take that as a sign to pull back.

"Tabitha, stop. I'm gonna come if you keep going."

She laughs, increases her speed. "Why would I stop?"

Next thing I know, I'm coming all over Poison Princess's hand.

"Oh, fuck, Tabitha, so good," I babble as she finishes me off. My body flops downward, my eyes close, and I'm more relaxed than I've been in ages. My breathing starts to slow when Tabitha releases me...until she inserts a finger into my open mouth.

"Clean me off," she says softly.

What the fuck? I open my eyes to see her looking at my mouth, her cheeks flushed, waiting for me to do as she says. Never one to keep a lady waiting, I go for it. While it's never been something I've thought about before, right now I'd rather be doing nothing other than sucking my own cum off her long, elegant fingers. Her chest heaves as she watches me, her mouth open as she pants out her breath. I lick the last of my cum off her palm, then tug her tightly against me.

"I think it's only fair that I taste you," I whisper against her lips.

Her voice is shaky as she replies, "I don't know. I'm—I'm not ready."

I push her hair behind her ear and place a soft kiss on her temple. "What do you mean?"

"It's embarrassing."

I kiss her softly. "You don't have to do anything you aren't ready for, but I want you to know that you don't have to be embarrassed by anything with me. Alright?"

Tabitha blows out a breath as she nods. She takes my hands in hers, steps back, and looks around before returning her gaze to me. "Where's your room? Unless you want to stand at the door all night."

I grin as I guide her toward the hall. "All night, huh?"

She stops. *Oh shit, did I say something wrong?*

She looks at the bag on the floor. "Can I put my groceries in your fridge?"

Chapter Thirteen

Tabitha

OH MY—*OH, YES*.

Henry and I sit on the edge of his bed. He kisses along my neck and runs his fingers through my hair. It feels so good. I didn't think having my *neck* kissed would be this enjoyable. I can only imagine what the naughty bits are like.

Henry pulls away from me, drops to the floor, and begins the long task of removing my boots. He smiles up at me as he undoes the first buckle, and he looks so sweet I can't help but smile back. I smooth his hair and cup his chin.

"You're such a good boy," I say.

Something flashes in Henry's eyes. *Hmm.* He continues his task, and when he's done, I guide him up to sit with me again.

"We're not having sex tonight," I say.

He laughs. "That's totally fine. I didn't think we were going to."

"I don't really know what I want to do yet. Can we just see what happens?"

"Tabitha—anything, or nothing, is fine. It's all up to you."

"But you *do* want me, right? You're sure?"

I *know* he wants me—I just want to hear him say it.

He looks at me as if I've gone mad. "Are you kidding?"

I pull my sweater over my head and toss it on the floor. "Do you want me, Henry?"

He slides his fingers under the hem of my shirt, and when he sees permission in my eyes, lifts it up and over my head. His warm hand trails down my bare arm.

I'm in front of him in only my bra. I can't believe I'm this nervous. When did I become such a wuss? I shake off my nerves. This is Henry, and I don't need to feel awkward with him.

I kiss Henry deeply. He gently pushes me back so I can lie with my head on the pillows, and positions himself between my legs. This feels very...right, somehow. How unexpected.

He presses his nose to mine and says, breathlessly, to me, "I want you so fucking much. I would do anything to have you. Anything *for* you. Every second I spend with you makes me want you even more."

Good enough for me. I lift the hem of his shirt, and he sits to pull it over his head. He looks good. *Great*, even. I slide my hand into his pants to find his cock, hard again, and stroke it for a bit. I think if he's super worked up, then maybe it'll be easier to get him to accept my weird body. That's my plan, anyway. Once he's fully getting into it, I let him go, reach behind me, and undo my bra. When I pull it off and toss it aside, I wait for Henry's reaction.

It's good. He licks his lips and tugs his pants down low enough to set his cock free. He strokes it as he gazes at my exposed breasts. He then lies flat against me, practically moaning into my ear, "Sorry to be vulgar, but you have the nicest tits I've ever seen."

The anxiety I'm feeling over that part is immediately released in a rush of breath. I run my hands over his back and ask, still a little self-consciously, "You don't think they're weird?"

He sits back up and raises an eyebrow. "Why? Are you just nervous because of the green nipples?"

I groan and reach for a pillow to cover my face. "Yes, the green nipples. Why did you say it like that?"

"Newsflash—nipples come in a lot of colors. Maybe not usually green, but I'm not worried about it. And holy *fuck,* your tits are..." Henry forms his hands into a praying pose and smiles toward the sky. "They're a miracle. A huge, bouncy, all-natural miracle."

"Yeah?" I can't help but crack a smile at the pervert.

"Absolutely." Henry lowers himself until his mouth is above the peak of my breast and grins before sticking out his tongue and dragging it across my hard nipple. I hum in delight at the feeling, but when he sucks it into his mouth, gently grazing it with his teeth, I moan.

"Oh, wow. That feels good." I grab him by his hair and lift him to look at me. "Henry—do that again."

With a nod and smile, he says, "Yes, ma'am," before returning to position.

He continues to kiss, lick, and suck my breasts until I'm writhing in the sheets. It feels amazing. But it's not enough.

"Henry, I need—I need—" I whine as I grip the bedding below me.

"What do you need? Anything, I'll give it to you."

"I need more. I feel like, I don't know, there's so much pressure building up inside me."

"Do you mean you want to come? Because I have absolutely no problem with making that happen."

I assess the feelings in my body, but that awkward self-consciousness sets in again. "I think so. Theoretically, anyway."

Henry looks at me, brow furrowed, before it hits him. "Are you saying that you've never—"

"I've never had an orgasm."

"Alright, I know other people can't touch you, but you can still touch yourself. When you were alone, why didn't you, you know... pet the kitty?"

I can feel my face scrunch up so hard with awkwardness that I could potentially implode. I slap my hands over my eyes and groan.

"I was too busy living a messed-up life and then being mentally unwell. I don't know. It just wasn't a priority. Plus, I guess, I just don't often feel sexual desire."

I peek through my fingers and see Henry smirking. "But you feel sexual desire for me?"

"You're going to get all cocky now, aren't you?"

"Oh, yeah. My dream woman can only get her pussy wet for me? Fuck yes, I'm gonna feel good about myself."

"Why did you have to say it like that? Aah!" I smack him with the nearest pillow.

He laughs. "So violent, all because you want me to touch your hot, wet pussy."

Okay, now I'm annoyed, because his saying that really *is* making me feel things between my legs. I whine in frustration.

Henry undoes the button on my pants smoothly, then unzips them. "It's alright. No need to be upset. Your first orgasm is gonna be amazing. Let me take care of it."

"Just—remember that I'm not normal."

"Whatever you are is what I want." Henry tugs off my pants—damn things are tight—and tosses them to the floor, leaving me in my black underwear. When he slips them off of me and spreads my thighs apart, I close my eyes and wait for his reaction.

"Wow," he says softly. "You're beautiful."

"I'm a freak."

"You're colorful."

I laugh. That's true. There are many shades of blue, yellow, and green splashed down there. But that's not the main issue.

"I don't even have a regular...yeah."

Henry crawls up to look at me face-to-face. "Well, tell me what's different, and I'll go with it. I've got the will to succeed."

"I don't even know what to do. How can you figure it out?"

"Tell me what you know and I'll, uh, start exploring. I love an adventure."

I rub my face nervously before I get into the explanation. "I hate you." I throw my bra at him, and he laughs. "Anyway, the, um, sensitive part that's on the outside of the vaginal entrance—"

"The clit?"

"Yes, but I hate saying it. Anyway, my *clit* is still tucked in above my vagina, but they screwed up, and

there are two of them that are kind of twined together,
I guess."

"You have two clits? How have you not come if
you have two?"

"It's uncomfortable and confusing, okay? Since
I don't get turned on often, they're just sensitive bits
there to annoy me."

"Well, I'm gonna try not to be annoying. In fact,
I plan on being quite the opposite." Henry says, his tail
wrapping around my ankle.

"You sure?"

"Yep." He kisses my stomach, my hip, then my
inner thigh.

I shake my head as he wiggles his eyebrows. "If
you insist."

"Oh, I do." He makes himself comfortable down
between my legs again. "I'm going to start doing different touches. Let me know if something feels good or
bad or meh."

"Okay." I clutch the sheets nervously and watch
as he kisses down my thigh. "You're very handsome."

"I know," he says before continuing his kisses all
the way to my center.

"Good," I say softly.

He kisses over a few different parts of my brightly
colored outsides, and it's mostly rated "meh." Next, I
hiss as he inserts the tip of his finger inside me.

"Bad."

He nods, kisses my knee, then squints at me as
if he's looking for something in my expression. When
he doesn't find it, he kisses my other knee and says, "If
we were about to fuck—don't worry, I know we aren't,
this is just a question—tell me how you'd want me."

"Oh, um, I guess I'd let you figure it out—"

"No, you tell me what you imagine. Say it out loud."

Suddenly, it feels like there's no saliva in my mouth, but I attempt to speak anyway. "I suppose the first thing I imagined when I thought of it was you behind me."

Henry rubs a place on my center that feels nice. I hum softly at the feeling of it, combined with the thought of having sex with him.

"In detail, Tabitha," he insists, stroking the good spot.

"We're both naked. I'm bent over a table. Your cock slams into me over and over." I moan as Henry inserts his finger inside me again. It slides easily into me this time. "Good. Very good."

"Tell me how much you want my cock, Tabitha."

I press my hips against Henry's hand, feeling that pressure from earlier build again. "I want it so much. It's so hard and smooth, and I want to rub it and suck it and, oh fuck, I want it inside me. Henry. Good, good, so good."

Then, he finds a spot inside that I didn't know existed. I grit my teeth as my toes curl, my hips raising from the bed, my leg muscles freezing. He rubs the spot inside while caressing my clits. My body pulses, a kind of euphoric explosion taking over me. It lasts for a million years, or maybe less than a minute, and then it's over.

"There we go," he says. "That wasn't so difficult."

I want to reply to him, smack him with a pillow, something, but all that comes out is a long wheeze. He kisses up my stomach, and when he's face-to-face with me, he nudges my nose with his. Somehow, I manage to work up enough energy to flip my floppy body onto its side and wrap my arm around him.

"That was highly enjoyable," Henry says.

"I would like more in the future, yes," I mumble into his shoulder.

"They're only gonna get better, you know that?" he says as he twirls a lock of my hair.

"Not possible."

He laughs and snuggles against me with his arms wrapped around my waist. "Stick around, and you'll find out."

"I feel sleepy. Maybe I should go home."

"Maybe you should stay the night. I can take you to your place in the morning."

I frown as I look at the nice sheets underneath us. "Your bedding is so destroyed. You know that, right? After all of my...*moisture* has been on it."

He smirks. "You mean when you came all over it?"

"You're annoying."

"Well, you said you wanted to suck my cock. I can't be that annoying."

I roll away from him and grab my sweater off the floor. "I'm going to use the restroom."

"I'm gonna think about your wet pu—"

I throw a pillow over his face to shut him up and head to the bathroom to do my business. When I get out, Henry shouts, "Hey, I'm in the kitchen! Come get a snack!"

As I am indeed hungry, I follow the instructions. When I get there, I discover he's making some kind of nacho thing. There is ground beef cooking on the stove. All sorts of dips and such. I recoil.

"I'm sorry, but I can't eat with you," I say.

Henry stands there looking concerned, spatula in hand. "Oh, is it a dietary issue? I can make something else. Or we can order in. There's a great pizza place over here."

I shudder at the thought of all of a fully-human stranger privately making me a dish with all sorts of ingredients layered together. "No, thank you. You can eat whatever you like. I'll just eat from my groceries."

"Are you sure? Because—"

"I really, really have to eat my groceries."

It's better to get this out of the way now, I suppose. While he finishes cooking, I take my bag out of the refrigerator and prepare my own food. I wash the oranges, give them a good scrub, and inspect them for any tampering before peeling them and placing them onto a plate in their individual sections. I open a bag of individually wrapped string cheese, unwrap two, and set them next to my orange slices. I wash and scrub a large carrot, peel it, then cut it into coin-sized slices, before setting them next to the string cheese. I crack open a can of sparkling water and pour it into a rinsed glass cup. Then, I sit down to eat.

Henry sits in front of his giant tray of nachos, staring at my plate. "That's all you eat?"

"I ate other stuff earlier today," I say before crunching a carrot coin.

"It's kind of a...I don't know. Are you trying to lose weight or something? Because you really don't—"

I hold up my hand to stop him. "Okay, rude. Some people are just particular about food. In my case, it's a trauma thing. Not a weight thing."

"Trauma makes you eat string cheese and carrots?"

It's rude as hell to comment on people's diets. Normally, I'd tell someone off, but he looks so genuinely confused, I can't help but want to explain.

"When I was being experimented on, they would sometimes slip drugs into our food. When I was in prison, it was even worse. There were people there whose families had died in the Mash-Up, or who were harmed themselves. They couldn't get revenge on Darkiss, so they saw me as the next best thing. The people in the kitchen used more than a few meals to torture me. I no longer trust anything that isn't perfect and untouched before I eat it."

"That's incredibly fucked up. I'm sorry."

"I understand why they hated me. The people at the prison, anyway. It's hard to blame them when so much of who I am is built on vengeance. The people at Geiger, however, can get fucked." I bite into an orange slice, the sweet juice squirting onto my tongue as my teeth pierce the thin membrane.

"I'll make sure to keep safe foods around for when you come over. Let me know what you need."

"Oh, you're really sure you've got me hooked now, huh?"

"Oh, yeah. You didn't see your face when you came, but I did. That was the face of a woman who's coming back for more." Henry shoves a chip into his mouth and wiggles his eyebrows.

"*Ugh.* I want to say I won't be, but I'd be lying. You don't have to look so smug about it, though."

"I'm just proud of a job well done. Wouldn't mind being hired on full-time."

His cheeks turn pink as he becomes suddenly very interested in watching himself move the chips back and forth on his plate, rather than looking at me.

"By that, do you mean fooling around forty hours a week, or was that a metaphor?"

He clears his throat, his eyes darting toward mine, then back to focus on his cooling nachos.

"Metaphor. Though spread out over seven days, forty hours sounds doable." He looks at me again with a cocky grin I can't help shaking my head at. "I just mean we could make us a thing. There's a connection here, and I'd really like to see where we can take this beyond the casual hook-up stage."

Wow. This is new. I look around the apartment for—not really sure what, actually, but something that proves this is real. I have my old friends. It's not beyond the realm of possibility that someone would be sexually attracted to me. But someone wanting to be in an *exclusive relationship* with me—and a kind, handsome, funny, smart, considerate man at that—doesn't make sense.

"Tabitha? I'm sorry if I'm moving too quickly. You can ignore me," Henry says, and I realize I've been quiet for an uncomfortably long time.

"No, it's okay. I'm just surprised. I'm used to people either hating me or being afraid of me. Occasionally, fetishizing me. Wanting to be in a committed relationship with me is unexpected." I look out of the kitchen, into the living room, and frown. "You'd have to put covers on everything every time I come over, just in case. I'll have to get you some of the special soap I use to keep here. There are different types for laundry, household cleaning, and for the shower. We'd have to make sure I'm not around when Mark's son is here. It'll be a big hassle, and you must take it seriously."

Henry's face perks up; he slaps one hand over his heart and raises the other. "I swear to take it very, very seriously. I will be doing so much laundry and cleaning, and will buy tons of extra sheets and sofa covers, and fancy soap. I'm gonna take so many extra showers. No one will ever be harmed because of how much I love your pussy. I promise."

"Oh my fucking god, why did you have to say it like that?" The orange slice I throw hits him on the end of the nose.

"Hey, now, you almost splashed orange juice in my eye. If I go blind, I won't be able to see your beautiful green nipples."

"*Ugh!*" I shove a string cheese into my mouth.

"It's tragic that you don't peel the cheese into little strings. It's *string* cheese. Not *shove in mouth whole cheese*."

I roll my eyes and decide to ignore that one.

After he eats another loaded chip, he wrinkles his nose. "Yeah, those are super cold and soggy. I think it's bedtime now anyway."

"I guess. As long as you can still take me home early so I can get ready for work."

Henry smiles warmly and takes my hand. "Of course."

I smile back but snatch my hand away. "You got hamburger juice on my hand. Sick. I'm gonna go wash it off, and I'll meet you for sleepy time."

Henry laughs and stands up. "Alright. I'll wash these dishes, then meet you there, my new girlfriend."

Girlfriend. Wow.

Chapter Fourteen

Henry

WE DID NOT GO to sleep right away. As soon as I saw her lying there, I had to kiss her. As soon as I kissed her, she had her hand in my boxers. Apparently, she really likes how my dick feels. Which I am *not* upset about. Not at all.

In the morning, I, of course, wanted to make her come before we left. Had to give her a good start to her first full day as my girlfriend. No slacking off for me!

Then, I took her to her apartment so we could each use her special soap. Sadly, she decided we needed to take separate showers and end the sexy stuff for the day.

After that, we went to work and pretended like we were just casual friends. Friends who can't even touch each other. At all. It was terrible. She barely acknowledged me. I had to wrap my tail up with packing tape because it kept going rogue on me and trying to touch her. When the workday was over, I was bursting with joy. I offered to drive her home, but she turned me down. I don't understand why she would want to take the bus instead of riding in a car with her *literal boyfriend*. It makes no sense.

So now I'm sitting on my sofa, with the TV on some random talk show I've never heard of, waiting for her to text me back. I feel like a pathetic teenager again, moody as fuck over a girl, but I don't care. If I must relive my emo phase to have my Tabitha, then so be it. Bring forth the skinny jeans and black hair dye, for I am all in on love.

One of the ladies hosting the show, the one with the exaggerated accent and round hair, says something that catches my attention.

"We have with us today a former member of the group of Villains who would become Darkiss's comrades. Please welcome Yvette, also known as Four Ever."

A woman I vaguely remember reading about, but have never seen, strolls onto the set, waving like a beauty pageant contestant. She must have started working for the government at some point because she's wearing a patriotic, Hero-coded costume.

It's not like there's a rule for what powered people can and can't wear—at least as far as I know. Well, maybe for the ones that work for the government, I guess. The rest of them just do what they want. The thing is, you can always tell by their final look where they stand. For example, a Hero would never have worn what Tabitha did. Her black cape and barely-there bodysuit are *so Villain*-coded. On the flip side, Tabitha would never be seen in the weird sparkly jumpsuit this lady on the TV is wearing.

Villains always have the better fashion sense.

"So, Yvette, before we begin, tell us what everyone wants to know," one of the other hosts, the petite one with all the plastic surgery, asks.

"What are my powers?" the guest asks, smiling with big, bright, white teeth at the cheering audience. "Well, my name says it all. I can make four of me."

The group gasps and cheers.

"Four? Like four clones? I wish I could make four of me so I wouldn't have to watch football with my husband. Oof," the host with the ugly shirt and former stand-up comedy career says.

Why do so many people make jokes about disliking their spouses or not enjoying time with them? If my partner didn't enjoy doing an activity with me, we just wouldn't do it together. It would hurt my feelings if they spoke poorly about our relationship on national television.

"Yes, sort of, except they get reabsorbed into me after about thirty minutes—sooner if I want."

"Maybe you can show us at the end of the interview?" Round Hair asks.

"Sounds great!"

The audience cheers.

"So, now, tell us about your time with Darkiss. What was he like?" Petite asks.

"Absolutely captivating, but terrifying, and—"

My phone buzzes. I scramble to find it on the sofa, eventually digging it out from between the cushions. I re-read my text to her, then her response with a relieved grin.

> **Me:** Hey, hey. You didn't want a ride?

"And then he said he wanted to teach the world a lesson. He would stop them from destroying each other and the planet by any means necessary. I knew what he could do, so I guessed what was going to happen. I tried to warn his harem before I left, but they wouldn't listen. Maybe if they had, he wouldn't have had the courage to go through with it," Yvette says on the TV, the exaggerated emotion on her face making me think some of her story isn't entirely true. Like referring to Tabitha and her friends as a *harem*.

"I don't know why those Deviants are free. Just walking about with you and me," Round Hair says.

"They're not like you at all," Petite says, setting her hands on top of the guest's. "You turned yourself into the police and began to work for the military."

"That's right. I was the last to be trained by the legendary Silent Shock."

"Those three wicked broads that hung around Darkiss should be locked up for good, in my opinion. Throw away the key. Put 'em all in the same little cell, even. Call it the Big Mash-Cell," the Comedian says.

Everyone on the TV is laughing when I turn it off. Fucking idiots. I bet they're the same people who hate Mashies, too. They just give off that vibe. Assholes.

I go to my room to play a game on the computer or something, blow off some steam. First, I gotta text Mark.

> **Me:** Don't forget tonight. Six.

He responds right away.

> **Mark:** How could I forget? It's just ANGELUST.

> **Me:** I see no issue

> **Mark:** You wouldn't. I'll be there.

I absolutely annihilate some zombies for a couple of hours, dick around online, jack off in the shower, and then get dressed. By the time I'm done getting ready for our double date, I look, smell, and feel better than I have in years. I even exfoliated my tail.

At fifteen minutes to six, my door buzzer goes off, and I jump off the sofa to answer it. My lady love enters my apartment shortly after, her friend in tow. Tabitha is covered head to toe as usual. I'm sure she's probably wearing pants underneath, but she's wearing a long, black dress, and I can pretend there's nothing under it if I want to. It's not a super fancy dress—I don't know the names of clothes, but it's a simple, flowy thing, made of a plain, soft material—and she's wearing a hooded shawl in the same fabric over it. It's gorgeous. She lowers the hood when she gets inside and smiles at me, her black eyes sparkling under the extravagant eyeliner she put on today.

"Ooh, you did makeup. It looks very pretty," I say as I walk over and wrap my arms around her. "And this dress is fantastic."

"I don't get to dress up often. Feels weird," Tabitha says.

"Hon, you look gorgeous. You should be feeling like a million bucks. Look at that figure of yours. Legs for days!" Angela says.

Tabitha waves her off, though her smile says she enjoys the compliment. "You should talk about a nice figure. Look at you!"

"Oh, but I know I look good. I don't need any reassurance. Always nice to hear it though." Angela winks, and her aura is such that I swear sparkles come out when she does so.

The door buzzes again, and I let Mark in while Tabitha sets up her special soap in my bathroom. When he gets inside—looking well-dressed and not frazzled for once—he slaps me on the back, and then his eyes lock onto Angela. I can see his pupils grow instantly, and his cheeks turn pink. *Oh, boy.* I slap him on the back and direct him further into the room.

"Mark, this is Angela. Angela, this is Mark."

Angela, dressed in a tiny red dress that shows off her hourglass figure, holds out her hand. Mark starts to reach for her, but hesitates. She looks at his paused hand and wiggles her well-manicured fingers.

"Mark, honey, I promise not to put you under. I can control it. It ain't like Tabby's poison. If you have any feelings in your heart or your pants tonight, it's all on you." She wiggles her fingers again.

Mark accepts her handshake, and Angela smiles, squealing and shrugging her shoulders in delight. *Oh, lord. She's catnip for Mark.*

"Are we going, or what?" Tabitha interrupts.

"Yep, everyone get out of my house," I say, pointing to the door.

The restaurant is a place I've never heard of, in an area I rarely go to. This neighborhood used to be pretty cool. It was artists and college students mostly. It got hit hard by structural damage in the Mash-Up, and since artists and college students don't have a ton of money, it got put at the end of the list when it came time to distribute funding. The whole place became kind of a slum, and the worse it got, the less people sought to improve it. I honestly didn't even know businesses were operating in this part of the neighborhood. Shows my bias, I guess.

The entrance doesn't make it obvious there's a restaurant here, to be fair. The windows are covered in metal screens, the sign is tiny, and the paint on it is wearing off. I can barely make out the pink retro letters that say "Sandra's Diner." It's not entirely clear whether or not it's even open. Tabitha walks right in, though. So, here I go too.

There is a Mashie standing at a hostess table looking at her phone when we walk in. At first, I'm not sure what kind of Mashie she is, but when the scent of the meat cooking fills my nostrils, it triggers something. I recognize the horns on her head and the spotted pattern on her skin.

How the *fuck* is a cow Mashie working at what certainly seems to be a hamburger joint? That's some twisted shit.

She lifts her head and smiles widely when she sees our group. She drops her phone and opens her arms wide.

"*Olá* Tabitha! Angela! *Que bom te ver!*" The woman does a sort of shimmy in front of Tabitha—obviously keeping a safe distance—but embraces Angela, giving her kisses on both cheeks. When they pull away from each other, the woman finally notices Mark and me. Her impeccably groomed eyebrows raise. Angela whispers something to her that has her glancing at Tabitha and raising her eyebrows even higher.

Tabitha crosses her arms and shoots Angela an annoyed look before stating in her monotone way, "*Gostaria de uma mesa pra quatro, por favor.*"

Now it's my turn to raise my eyebrows.

"Hey, I didn't know you could speak..." I realize I don't know what language that is. Fuck, I took a different mandatory language in school because there were a bunch of super cute girls in the class. I don't even remember any of it, aside from asking where the bathroom is.

"I can't," Tabitha finishes when it becomes obvious I can't. "I only know a little because Alice is forcing me to learn. She's very annoying!"

Cheerful Alice is entirely unfazed. Smiling, she waves four menus at us. We head into the dining room, which is much nicer than I expected it to be from the outside, I must say. I start to reach for Tabitha's hand, but catch myself before it's too late. Not touching her in public is going to be tougher than I thought.

We get seated, and I look around at all the happy people at the pink tables. Everyone looks delighted, having fun, drinking milkshakes.

Wait. Those aren't normal people. They're Mashies. Well, most of them are *visibly* Mashies. Some might be regular people, some might have hidden animal parts. Either way, it's weird to see so many of *us* in one place.

An elbow suddenly jabs me between two ribs. *Ouch.*

"Stop staring," Tabitha hiss-whispers. "Answer the server."

A tall, handsome man with skin and hair nearly as dark as Tabitha's cloak, and an impressive rack of antlers, waits for my answer to a question I didn't hear. His adorable black deer nose, with the tiniest bit of white fur at the end, twitches in annoyance.

My cheeks heat in embarrassment as I apologize. "Ah, I'm sorry. Can you repeat that?"

"May I have your drink order?"

"Oh, yeah, of course. Just water. Thanks." When the waiter walks away, I excitedly turn to the people at my table and say as quietly as I can, "There are so many Mashies here. This is crazy. I hardly ever run into more than one Mashie a week, let alone this many at once."

Tabitha and Angela smile at each other before looking back at me.

Tabitha says, "Yeah, I'm sure you're aware there are still a lot of places that aren't fond of the more visible Mashies in their places of business. These places where they can be themselves have been such a refuge for so many people who don't have anyone in their lives to have their backs. You have Mark, and you work in a normal job, but not everyone has been so lucky."

Angela nods solemnly. "They welcome everyone, not just Mashies. As long as you're accepting of them, they'll accept you. When we first got out of prison, we couldn't go anywhere without getting told we weren't welcome. Still have a hard time finding a friendly face. But Alice invited us right in."

"Wow, that's really cool. I'm happy there are people like her in the city." I watch her laugh with a couple across the dining room.

Both of the women at the table with Alice have highly visible cat features. The ears, whiskers, slitted pupils, and even the pink noses couldn't be hidden away like my tail. Alice certainly couldn't hide either. Not with those cute little horns and the patterned skin. One of the ladies in the couple takes a bite of a burger, and I can't help but cringe. I have to say something, it's just so odd.

I lean into the group and say quietly, "It's weird that she's a cow Mashie that runs a burger joint, right? Is it cannibalism? I suppose if that's what she was used to doing before the Mash-Up, then—"

"Fucking hell, Henry!" Tabitha snaps.

"What?" I look at her, confused.

"They don't sell beef or dairy here," Angela says, covering her face with a napkin to hide her smile.

"It smells like it, though! Right, Mark?"

He lifts his hands to his sides. "Leave me out of this."

I toss a napkin at him. "Ugh, traitor."

Angela and Tabitha look at each other. Tabitha shrugs, then Angela tells me about Alice.

"It's a *vegan* restaurant. It didn't used to be, but Alice bought the place for cheap after the Mash-Up, kept the original name and decor, but converted the recipes. She used to be the owner of a super fancy farm-to-table restaurant in one of the ritzy suburbs. They got their vegetables, meat, milk, and eggs all from local farms. She would visit them to make sure the livestock were well-kept and everything. That's how she ended up with the whole—" Angela mimes horns, "—thing. A lot of Mashies understandably developed a strong distaste for any animal products after the Mash-Up, including her, so she closed her old restaurant and opened one here, where there are more Mashies. The scent is a very convincing meat substitute."

Tabitha pokes a finger at my menu. "If you would look at your menu, you'd know that. Less yapping, more reading."

"Well, golly, forgive a man for wanting to talk to his sexy, beautiful, goddess of a date," I say as I pick up my menu.

Tabitha picks up hers and mumbles, "I mean, it's okay if you talk while reading. Whatever."

Mark and Angela quietly snicker, hiding their grins behind their menus. All of us go back to perusing the offerings. Everything looks pretty good. It's classic diner food, which I love and want to eat all of, so the decision is tough. When the waiter comes back, I still haven't decided, so I just quickly pick the first thing that comes to mind.

"Uh, can I get the double cheeseburger, extra pickles, and fries, with a strawberry shake.

Tabitha just orders cut fruit—even though Alice comes over and lectures her about being afraid of her kitchen—then Angela and Mark each order the burger, fries, and shake combo too.

It arrives pretty fast. Tabitha inspects my fries several times as I'm eating. I'm wondering if something is wrong, and I almost ask her if there is. Instead, I'm pleasantly surprised when she asks me to put one on her plate. She looks at it warily for a moment—the rest of us carefully trying not to let her see us watching her—then swiftly snatches it up and pops it into her mouth. She keeps the same grouchy look on her face that she normally has in public, so it's hard to know what she thinks, until finally she says, "Can I have another one?"

I throw several more onto her plate. When Tabitha isn't looking, I give Alice a thumbs up. The cow Mashie looks positively elated as she skitters into the kitchen. As soon as the double doors close, I hear a muffled whoop of joy that brings a grin to my face.

"What happened?" Tabitha says, looking at me as she munches away on her fried, starchy root.

"Nothing. Just happy to be here with my awesome girlfriend and you other two."

I look at Mark and Angela, and my eyebrows raise. The two of them are getting *very close.* Mark is whispering in her ear, and either she's on his lap or at the very least has a leg draped over him.

Tabitha looks at me and sighs. "If they end up having sex, I hope you know I'm going to hear every detail. She's very kiss and tell with Klaire and me. But yeah. Just know, I'll know all about your brother's dick skills if it comes to that, whether I want to or not. And for the record, I do not."

"Eew. I did not want to hear the phrase 'your brother's dick skills' come out of the mouth of my hot date." I shudder. "Are you gonna share all our sexcapades with them?"

"Yeah."

"Aww, man. I don't know if I should feel violated or not."

"If it helps, I've only said good things so far. They were impressed that I came the first time I had a pants-off situation with a guy. I guess that's not normal. Klaire called you *The Magic-Fingers Marsupial*." She shrugs as my face turns hot enough to cook the fries.

"I guess that helps a little."

"We spent a lot of years together. Expect secrets to be shared. It's part of the territory." Tabitha takes a drink of water while I let that sink in. She sets down her glass, pats her mouth with her napkin, and smiles softly at me. "Klaire can read your mind anyway, Henry. You got into a mess when you decided to date me. Sucks to be you."

Something about that makes me laugh, just a little at first. Then harder when Tabitha looks at me, confused. When she joins in, I'm positively rolling. Henry and Angela break their little connection to look at us, and even they start giggling. I laugh until I'm in tears and my stomach muscles hurt. When I can't laugh anymore, and I'm running out of breath, I let my head fall back in my chair and smile up at the lights.

"Okay, so, why are we laughing?" Tabitha asks.

"I don't know. I guess it's how this feels so... normal? It's like, 'Oh yeah, the mind reader—my murderer girlfriend's best friend—will know all about my dick game.' And I'm—" I sit up straight and shrug, "totally fine with it. I've never been this happy. My bossy-ass, crabby girlfriend is fucking amazing. Her friends are awesome, and they like me too, I think."

"We do!" Angela says as she claps and bounces in her seat.

"See?" I point to Angela. "My brother likes my girlfriend, and her friends, and they all like him. Even my little nephew thinks my girlfriend is cool."

I turn to Mark and hold up my glass of water. "And he stays a safe distance away."

Mark laughs and holds his glass up to meet mine. "Cheers to that."

"I'm not that bossy," Tabitha grumbles around a mouthful of fried potato. "And we have yet to determine if there will be any dick games between us."

I laugh at Tabitha's comment and watch as Angela whispers something into Mark's ear. His eyes flutter closed, his mouth silently forming the word "fuck." Yeah, he's a goner.

Tabitha clears her throat then raises her hand to call Alice over. "May we have the check? I think my friends are ready for bed."

Alice looks at Mark and Angela, who've given up on manners and are full-on making out now like goddamn horny teens. Her eyebrows raise as she mumbles something under her breath, then pulls the check from her apron and sets it on the table.

"Pay me at the front when you're ready," she says before giving the lusty couple one more glance.

"Mark!" I snap.

He and Angela pull apart, looking rumpled and surprised, then slightly chagrined. Mark smooths his hair and clears his throat before replying.

"Sorry. Got carried away. Are we ready to go?"

"Yes. Got the check here." I hold it up so he can see.

He holds his hand out. "I'll cover it."

I frown. I know it's toxic, but my masculinity cannot allow another man to pay for my girlfriend's meal. How dare he even offer, frankly.

"I'll cover our half, you cover yours," I say, staring him dead in the eye so he knows not to argue.

Mark shrugs in acknowledgment. Angela puts cash on the table for the tip, despite Mark and me trying to stop her so that we could do it.

When we get to the desk to pay, Angela steps in front of us, touches my wrist, and tells me to give her the check. I immediately do as she says, no questions asked, because Angela's wish is my command.

She then tells Alice she is going to pay the entire bill. Mark's protest is quickly cut off when she touches her hand to his. Alice runs her credit card, and a moment later, we all leave.

Once we're outside, Angela's spell breaks. I shake my head and yell a bunch of gibberish in frustration. *Angela's wish is my command?!* Son of a bitch! A few passersby look at me like I'm crazy, which is fitting, because I feel crazy.

"What the hell? Don't do that!" I shout.

Angela shrugs one shoulder, tosses her hair, and begins the walk back toward my apartment. "You would have tried to keep me from paying, and I'm not about to debase myself by arguing with a man. Yuck."

I tug at my hair in frustration as I stand on the cracked sidewalk, watching Tabitha join her. "What does that even mean?"

Mark sighs and smiles as he watches them, then slaps me on the back. "They're goddesses, brother. They do not argue with us mortals. Accept it."

I shove him away from me, then march towards the ladies, Mark laughing as he follows me. "You're high on Angelust."

"Absolutely," he says. "It's fantastic."

Tabitha looks over her shoulder, black eyes shining in the streetlights. When she sees me coming toward her, her perpetual frown turns into a smile. All the frustration from the moment before disappears, and all that's left is her.

My goddess.

Chapter Fifteen

Tabitha

Mark drove Angela back to his place, and I have a feeling they're going to be there for a while. Good for them.

"What do you want to do now? Do you want me to drive you home, or do you want to hang out for a while?" Henry asks as we stand awkwardly in his living room.

"I would like to stay, if that's what you want."

He perks up, then finally sets his keys on the counter. "Alright, good. What do you want to do? We can watch some movies. I bet you missed a lot when you were in prison. Or—"

"Let's do lots of touching. Sexy stuff." I take off my cloak and toss it on the sofa.

"I am okay with that choice of activities," Henry says as he removes his jacket.

Excitedly, I pull my dress off over my head. I've been waiting all night for this reveal. I throw the dress toward the sofa without even paying attention to whether it lands there, only to whether Henry is looking at me.

He very much is.

"Is that..." He trails off, mouth still, but his eyes move across every inch of my body.

"Yes, it is," I answer.

His incomplete question was obvious. *Is that your Villain costume?*

I haven't worn it in a decade, and I've lost some weight since then, but it fits well enough. There isn't much to it. I don't have the cape on, so all that's left is the tiny swimsuit-like bodysuit holding my bits and bobs in place. Then, there are the matching bracers, and, finally, my black thigh-high boots.

I slip a finger underneath one of the upper straps of my bodysuit and run it slowly back and forth along the hard skin of my nipple. Henry's tongue darts out to wet his lips as he watches, his eyelids heavy, and his chest rising and falling quickly.

"Are you just gonna stand there and look?" I ask.

I plant my feet spread slightly wide, put one hand on my hip, and the other cupping my breast—the same pose as the poster on his bedroom wall. His breath catches, and he rubs his eyes.

"I'm afraid to move and break whatever illusion this is."

"Shut up and get over here before I get bored and go home," I respond drily.

"Don't have to tell me twice," he says, approaching me with eyes focused on my barely-covered chest.

When he reaches me, he drops to one knee, pushes a strip of fabric to the side, and takes my nipple into his eager mouth.

"Oh, I like that," I moan. I grab hold of his hair to guide him. "Henry, you're so good to me. Such a good boy."

I don't know why those particular words came out of my mouth. As soon as they're out, however, I know they're right.

Henry stills, kneeling before me, mouth open, hot breath on my wet breast. He takes hold of my hips, raises his head, and softly, with a raspiness to his voice, says, "Say it again."

It takes me a second to understand. He looks so *desperate*. But if that's what he wants, then I'll do it.

"You're a good boy, Henry."

His eyelids flutter as he exhales harshly. *Okay, yep, he liked that.*

The look on his face is *incredible*. It's making me feel things I haven't felt in a long time. Powerful and in control.

And no one is dying, so that's good.

I tug his hair back so he's facing me. He looks at me how people look at Angela when she has control of them. I feel a rush go from my chest all the way through my stomach that finally settles heavily and hotly between my legs. *Fuck, I like this.*

"Are you gonna be a good boy for me tonight?" I ask, my stomach tightening nervously with excitement.

"Yes," he rasps out. "I'll be good."

I lean down so I'm face-to-face with Henry, lick his bottom lip, and say, in the sultriest voice I can manage without feeling silly, "Why don't you prove yourself, then we can go to the bedroom. You'll find out what kinds of treats good boys get."

He doesn't take long to react, lifting one of my legs over his shoulder, fitting his head between my legs, and slipping his fingers inside me in less than thirty seconds. It's embarrassing how wet I was when he slipped the fabric aside to expose me, how easily he slid inside.

Shyness briefly overcomes me, makes me want to hide my face, but unfortunately, I don't have anything to lean against. I'm standing one-legged, holding onto this man for dear life.

"Fucking fuck fuck fuck fuck," he whisper-mumbles happily down there between licks and sucks.

It's kind of... adorable? Like a tiny kitten meowing happily as it eats food for the first time. I have to bite my lip to keep from laughing.

When he hits my trigger spot deep inside, I bite my lip even harder. He works against my soft flesh rhythmically until I'm panting and moaning. When he finally gets me over the edge, I come shouting his name with his hair gripped between my fingers.

As I come down, thighs shaking, he looks up at me questioningly. I pat him on the head, then gesture toward the hallway.

"Come on and get your treat."

I hear him laugh behind me as I walk toward the bedroom. To be honest, I have no idea what's about to happen, and I'm okay with that. I feel comfortable enough with Henry to improv.

When he enters the room, lifting his shirt over his head, I frown at the bandages that wrap his tail around his torso.

"Henry?"

He pauses with his shirt still in his hand. "Yes?"

"Next time you're with me, don't wrap your tail. Or, any time, for that matter. You shouldn't have to make yourself uncomfortable like that."

He nods once, closes his eyes, takes a deep breath, and nods again. Then, he continues undressing. The shirt and tail wrappings go into the wicker hamper, along with his pants and socks. I lean back and enjoy my little show.

When he's down to his underwear, he kneels before me. Using his teeth, he unzips each of my boots for me. I can barely breathe from the force of the heavy lust in his eyes. He slides the boots off and sets them carefully next to the bedroom door. He surprises me by kissing each of my toes until I'm in tears from giggling.

"I'm supposed to be giving you a treat, and yet you're the one being sweet," I say as we lie on the bed facing each other.

He tucks my hair behind my ear and nudges my nose with his. "Treat? Every day with you is a rare delicacy unlike any other."

"What am I supposed to say to something like that?"

"Nothing."

He kisses me slowly and deeply as we take off our remaining garments. The feeling of our bodies pressed entirely together, all that bare skin, is sinfully decadent to me after so much time starved of touch.

When I feel something rub against my vagina, I flinch, not because it's unwelcome—though I *am* unprepared—but because his cock is pressed against my stomach, and his hands are also accounted for. I have no clue what's touching me. I look between us to see what's going on and laugh at what I find.

"Oh, sorry," Henry says, his naughty tail slithering behind him.

"It's okay, it just surprised me." Butterflies threaten to overwhelm the delicate ecosystem of my stomach, but I surge forward with what I want to say anyway. "I wouldn't mind if your tail decided to do some exploring, though."

"Yeah?"

"In fact, I wouldn't mind if any part of you wanted to... explore." My face scrunches up as I cringe. That didn't go how I expected.

Henry pushes the hair off my forehead. "I think you should say outright what you want to say. If you're ready for it, then you can say it."

Argh. Okay. I need to psych myself up. None of this fragile, nervous stuff. I'm a badass bitch. I spent time in prison. I can say adult words. Let's go.

I lay my hand on his shoulder, look him in the eye, shove him to his back, and straddle him in one swift movement. Henry smirks, grabs my hips, and gives them a tight squeeze. Before I can lose my nerve looking down into his beautiful eyes, I let it out.

"I'm ready to have sex. Tonight." I clear my throat. *I got this.* "With you, obviously."

He grins. "Hopefully it's me."

I slap his chest, and he winces.

"That was my favorite nipple!"

"Well, don't be a smart ass then!"

"Fine. Carry on."

"Yes, I'm ready. Just to get everything out of the way, I can't get pregnant. I don't have any STIs, and I can't even get any, to my knowledge, if you're worried about that sort of thing. One of the very few benefits of being part frog, I suppose."

"Good to know. I'm mostly concerned about you having a good time. I want you to be comfortable."

"I'm fine. Just don't be weird about it."

"I'll do my best." Henry smiles softly and runs his hands up and down my waist. "Come back here."

"Fine."

We lay next to each other and kiss some more. When the heat is high again, Henry gently inserts his fingers inside me, letting me get used to two, then three, spreading them and stretching me, all the while making sure I'm comfortable.

When it's been long enough that I feel like I could handle him, I lift his face so that his eyes line up with mine, and say, "I'm ready now."

Henry nods, kisses me again, then positions us so that I'm on my back and he's between my legs. As he inserts the head of his cock into me, I inhale sharply.

He pauses, looks up at me, and says, "You have to relax and breathe. Okay?"

I exhale as I nod and let my muscles loosen. Henry continues sliding slowly into my pussy. It doesn't hurt like I worried it would. The pleasure I get from the soft, breathy sounds Henry makes as he's entering me distracts me from any potential negative feelings either way. And the quiet "*Fuck,*" he lets out when he's finally all the way inside? Absolutely *delicious*.

"Are you okay?" he asks, a shakiness to his voice.

"Very much so," I reply, a wobble to my own.

"Tell me if I need to stop."

"You know I don't mind bossing you around. I like it, even."

"I do know that, actually."

And then, we're having sex. I didn't think I'd ever do it, but here I am. Doing *it*. And *it* feels *good*. He doesn't go too fast or too hard, just keeps pace with our kisses. He tells me how beautiful I am, and that my pussy is the best he's ever had. I don't know if it's true, but I like hearing it. I'm certainly starting to appreciate having two clits because the *holy shit* every time one of them gets rubbed it's... yeah. Wow. I really like touching.

At one point, he lifts one of my legs, far enough that my knee is touching my ear. His cock hits that wonderful part way inside of me that I love when his fingers get to. My eyes practically roll back in my head.

"Do that again. Right there."

Thankfully, he listens. He finds the spot again and rolls his hips just right, hitting it in a way that's even better than with his fingers because all his weight is behind it. He lifts my other leg, and now he's also grinding hard against my clits.

It's almost too much. I feel like I'm going to come, but at the same time, I don't think I should because it's *too* intense. There's a weird feeling, like—I don't know. Something's going on. I press his shoulder to tell him to stop, but the look on his face gives me pause. I've never seen him look like that; he's in absolute rapture. I guess I'll give it another second to see if— no—*oh, fuck,* I really need to tell him to stop.

"Henry. I—I think I'm gonna p—"

He kisses me hard before I can finish my sentence. I wriggle underneath him, but it only manages to make the sensations stronger. And then, I come harder than I knew was possible.

I can't hear anything, I can't move, nothing matters but his cock in my cunt. It feels so fucking incredible that I can't be embarrassed about the liquid gushing from between my legs.

Henry's certainly not stopping because of it. If anything, he seems weirdly excited, because when it happens, he looks between us and lets out the filthiest groan I've ever heard, before grabbing hold of my hips and fucking me like a maniac.

I have no idea what's going on. While being bounced silly by Henry, I try to catch a breath. When I can finally form words, I say, "Should we stop? Something happened when I came."

To my surprise, Henry *laughs*. He kisses me hard and moans into my mouth. He loses his rhythm, groans my name against my lips, and adds to my wet mess. His movements steadily slow, and after another moment, he stills, rubs his nose against mine, and smiles.

"You okay, Tabitha?"

"Yeah, except I peed the bed."

He laughs again. *Getting real sick of those laughs.*

"You did *not* pee the bed."

I shove him off me, wincing when his softening cock slides out, and gesture to the soaked sheets. "Look!"

Henry wraps his arms around me and pulls me against him. "Not pee."

I shove him off me again. "You're crazy."

"I thought you were the big, bad, prison lady. Didn't you talk about sex stuff there? It's not pee, Tabitha. You just, you know…" He makes an explosion sort of motion with his fingers near his dick, then sticks his tongue halfway out in a perverted way that makes me want to spray him with pepper spray.

"In case you forgot, I was not exactly a hot date. No one was talking to me about sex in prison. If anyone was near me, they were likely trying to shank me. Also, I spent a lot of time in solitary. Most of it, in fact. I mean, Klaire and Angela talked about stuff around me, but, honestly, I blocked out the explicit details. It kind of made me sad, since I didn't think I'd ever get to experience it. It's pathetic, same as always. Okay? What you're showing me now doesn't help, by the way, since I don't know what exploding dick has to do with me."

Henry grabs me again, and this time, while I growl at him, I don't shove him away.

"You squirted. It's just an uncommon type of orgasm. That's it. No big deal. But I'm sorry you're having weird feelings after your first time. If I can make it better somehow, let me know."

I head butt him lightly, rest my cheek against his, then wrap my arms around his shoulders.

"Eh. Besides the weirdness at the end, it was great. I think I'd even do it again sometime."

"Oh, really?" Henry pulls back to look at my face and grins when he finds me smiling at him. "Well, I think I'd like to join you, if you'd allow it."

"I'll allow it. Next time, let's start earlier so that we don't have to get up for work in the morning."

Henry's face falls. "Ugh. Do we have to go?"

"We can't both call out sick."

He flops backward into the mattress. "Tell them I died. Then you can call in sick."

"Very funny." I pull him up by the arm and press a quick kiss to his nose. "Now, let's get cleaned up because you'll have to take me home really, really, ridiculously early before work. Sorry."

"Ugh, annoying." He runs his fingers through my hair. "You're lucky I love you."

Both of us freeze. I clear my mind so that I don't make assumptions about what I just heard. If I think about it...I don't know what that could lead to. I can't react before I know what he meant. I'll wait for him to say something first. That way I'll have the facts before I say something and—

"Yeah," he says, letting out a long breath. He lifts my chin so he can look me in the eyes. "I love you. I wanted to wait to say it, when I thought you were for sure ready to hear it, but my mouth went rogue. It's as bad as my tail, I guess. So, that's that—I love you."

Okay. Having all the facts doesn't make it easier to know what to say. I guess the only thing to do is what I always do—tell him the truth.

"I don't know if I love you," I say. The hopeful light in his eyes starts to flicker, so I grab hold of his hands and squeeze them tightly. "It doesn't mean I don't. I just don't know what it means. How would I know?"

Henry's brow scrunches as he lowers our hands. He guides me to lie down on the bed, and we snuggle together under the covers, in the dry area. When he's behind me, holding me snug, he finally answers.

"I don't think I can tell you how you'll know if you're in love, Tabitha. At some point, you'll be with someone and realize that they mean everything to you. You would do anything, give anything for them. They feel like they belong in your world, and you in theirs, and without them, it wouldn't be complete. You just... know." He wraps his tail around my thigh and squeezes. "Though I think my tail knew before the rest of me."

I laugh and snuggle into the crook of his arm. Do I love Henry? I've spent so long feeling rage, isolation, and shame that I think it'll take me a while to know. Hopefully, he'll understand.

A soft snore comes from behind me, Henry's gentle breath caressing my neck. Okay, well, I guess he's not too upset about it right now. We'll talk about it later.

Chapter Sixteen

Henry

"Well, looks like we'll be closed tomorrow. They moved up the date of Honor Man's wedding. I guess the day and location they advertised were fake all along. How about that?" Milly tells us as we walk in, bleary-eyed, the next morning.

"Wait, what? Why are we closed for his wedding?" Tabitha asks.

"They need all the stores in the area in a three-block radius of Capital Square closed for the ceremony. They expect a huge crowd, and they need tight security." Milly shrugs. "Maybe in case there's some kind of threat."

"That's stupid. No one is going to interrupt his dumb wedding. The only one who even cares is Darkiss—" Tabitha starts.

"Tabitha!" Milly says as if her saying his name will summon him.

Tabitha continues, "—and he's freaking brain dead. It's a waste of taxpayer money. As someone who is paying taxes for once, I finally get to complain."

"Well, I'm going to watch the wedding. I think it's exciting. He's marrying a normal lady, just like us." Milly clasps her hands under her chin with a faraway romantic look in her eyes, but when she notices the doubtful look in Tabitha's eyes, she drops her hands. "Well, like me."

"I think we should watch it, Tabitha. Mashies and ex-villains are part of the community too," I say, sending her a wink when Milly claps happily at the idea.

"Oh, you should. Oh!" Her eyebrows raise, and she reaches into her apron pocket. After shuffling a few things around in there, she pulls out a key ring. "You can watch up on the roof, so Tabitha doesn't bump into anyone! Just don't let anyone know I gave it to you."

I take the key ring from her and hold it above my head, wiggling it and smiling at Tabitha. "Don't worry, Milly. We can't even get into the store with this key, just the outer stairwell. What could go wrong?"

Tabitha frowns and crosses her arms. "Let's get to work. There's toilet paper with your name on it."

Milly giggles and pats me on the back. "Oh, you two are silly. I'm so glad you get along."

"Yeah, we get along pretty well," I say as I follow Tabitha out the door. She shoots me a '*Shut the fuck up*' look that has me grinning all the way to the back room.

The rest of the workday goes on as usual. We pretend we're not thinking about fucking the shit out of each other. We don't touch each other, except the few times my tail goes rogue and slips under her hoodie—thankfully, we catch it before anyone sees. The only times we talk are work-related. It makes it easier not to flirt. While we're alone back here most of the time, people do still occasionally come through. Don't want to be caught off guard.

When the day is over, I head to my car, and she heads toward the bus stop, which is where I ultimately pick her up. It's a huge relief to relax around her when her curmudgeonly ass flops into the front seat of my car.

"My place or yours?" I ask.

"Eh, mine. I should eat the vegetables before they go bad."

"Save the veggies, got it."

We head to her apartment, she eats a plate of a variety of evenly chopped raw vegetables—not even any dip, ugh—and I eat a sandwich I have delivered. Afterward, she takes a shower while I dick around on my phone, then I take a shower while she watches the news. The whole thing feels very "normal couple," and I kind of like it.

When I get out of the shower, I slide next to her on the sofa and drape my arm over her shoulder. She's sitting very straight, which makes the fact that she's a little taller than me more obvious. My statuesque beauty.

"So, what's new in the world, my love, my life, my everything?" I ask.

"So corny," she replies without looking my way. "As far as the news, there's some crackdown on re-formed Villains. It's weird. They're saying the ones they rounded up are all criminals, but I know some of those guys, and I don't believe it. They even took Diamond and Jakob Washington in for questioning, according to sources, which is insane. I know that Di-amond has been vocal about her issues with how the government handles powered people, but Jakob? He's one of their own. Like, high-ranking military. Doesn't make sense."

I must admit, as much as I have fetishized Superheroes—and yes, it was problematic, I'll admit it now—I haven't kept up with current political issues around them, unless it was in the Tabitha forums or a major news story. Which is also a problem, and another thing I'm going to need to work on if I'm gonna be with her. I need to make sure I know what's going on in her world.

"I have to admit, I'm not sure who Diamond and Jakob are," I say.

Tabitha looks at me like I'm a moron before turning back to the TV and deigning to reply to me.

"Diamond Washington is Silent Shock's real name. I don't know her personally or anything, but I know *of* her. I thought everyone did. She's probably the strongest Hero in Capital City, but since she's not a propaganda puppet like Honor Man, she always takes the backseat. Jakob is her son, also known as Captain Howl. They're ridiculously famous Heroes, so I assumed you'd know them, considering your whole—" she looks me up and down before making a jacking off motion, "you know."

I gasp in exaggerated offense.

"Hey now, I'm a very specific type of pervert. I like sexy, strong, tall, angry, vigilante types. But, whatever, now I know. So, the government is acting shady. That's nothing new. Right?"

"Yeah, I guess. It's just odd because they were trying so hard to convince the public that we Villains were reformed, and that there was nothing to worry about. It was a huge campaign. Now they're making all of these big, public, shady arrests. They don't do showy things like this for no reason. As one of their most famous catches, I'm feeling on edge here. I don't know. Maybe I'm paranoid."

"Hey. We'll stick together. As long as we don't go anywhere sketchy, we'll be fine." I pull her in for a hug. "Someday I'm going to take you away from the city. We'll go somewhere we can openly touch each other without worrying about getting kidnapped."

"Well, leaving the city would mean breaking the law," she says with a defeated sigh. "I'd have to go on the run forever."

"Then we go on the run."

Tabitha looks up into my eyes. "You'd do that for me?"

"Like I said last night—I'd do anything for you. *Anything,* Tabitha."

Tabitha gently strokes my cheek before standing. She reaches out for my hand, and I accept. We walk to her tiny bedroom where she strips before me, standing gloriously nude, the partial daylight seeping through the closed shades and highlighting colors on her skin I haven't yet seen, areas I haven't explored. I move to touch her, but she stops my hand and directs me to undress instead. My clothes hit the floor fast, and once I'm naked, I reach for her. Once again, she stops my hand. She surprises me by reaching for my tail.

"What have you tried with this?" she asks.

"Uh...what do you mean? Besides what we did together last night? That's about it."

Tabitha kisses the tip of my tail and slowly strokes it, as if it were a part of me that I'd rather she were stroking.

"I'm wondering if you've ever used it on yourself," she asks before sucking on it.

My eyes open wide in surprise. "Do you mean have I fucked myself with my own tail? Like in my ass?"

She smiles and shrugs, continuing to stroke the damn thing. *What the hell?*

"No! I have not. Give me my tail back." I attempt to yank my opossum part away, but she holds tight.

"I think we should try it," she says, pressing herself against me and pushing me forward until I fall back.

We land on the bed, and she straddles my hips, my tail still in her hand. She begins to rotate her hips in slow, small circles so that her soft, wet pussy grinds against my cock.

"I want you to fuck me while you fuck yourself with your tail."

"You mean fuck *you* with it?"

"No."

I hold onto her with my tail as she sucks the tip of it. A shiver runs through me as I accept the inevitable—I'm gonna do it, because I'll do whatever this perfect creature wants. That tail is going right into my ass, no questions about it. It leaves her mouth with a *pop* when she hears my sigh of acceptance, and is replaced with a wide grin. Her hips shimmy in excitement.

Well, here we go. From now on, if I'm gonna get freaky, it's gonna be with the woman I love every time. I grab her hips, digging my fingers into the strong muscle there, and flip us over. She yelps and giggles underneath me.

If she wants to play games, however, I'm gonna win. I get two inches away from kissing her before stopping and snapping my teeth. She stops giggling, holding her breath. When I speak, my voice is lower, my words steadier than they were a moment before.

"Come on, you nasty girl. Get on all fours if you want to fuck like an animal."

Tabitha swallows thickly, her eyes flicking back and forth quickly before she slowly rises. I sit up just enough for her to turn over and get awkwardly into position. I hum in appraisal before pressing her waist lower and lifting her ass. She exhales sharply. When I spread her cheeks apart, she reaches back to slap my hand away. I catch it with a laugh.

"Don't worry, I'm just looking. I'm not gonna do anything."

"Looking is weird anyway," she whines.

"Considering what I'm about to do to myself, not really."

"That's different. That's hot."

I run my hands along the firm globe of her ass and appreciate the view before me. "I think we're both very lucky in that department."

One issue we're going to run into is lubrication. I'm definitely not inexperienced in the anal department, and my tail is nicely tapered, but a guy's still gotta have a little help. I look around her room for something, *anything*, and find lotion next to the bed.

It's not ideal, but I'll do it for my freaky froggy.

I sneakily snatch it with my tail while I distract Tabitha by nibbling on her neck. As I stroke her pussy with one hand, I squirt the mango-scented lotion into my other. I know I shouldn't be embarrassed to do this—in fact, I should be open about this with my partner—but for this first time, I just don't want to get into the details. So, sue me.

I dip a finger into her slippery, neon-colored cunt. "Are you ready for my cock in that wet little slit?"

She mewls in the hungriest way that has my hips twitching and my heart pounding.

"Yes, please, fuck me now," she begs, shoving herself backwards against me.

"*Mmm,* like a bitch in heat," I grit out as I roughly jam the first hard inches inside her.

She moans and catches her breath before looking back at me. "That's such a fucked-up thing to say."

I grin, shoving myself nearly all the way in, watching her mouth pop open with pleasure. "Don't worry, I'll feed your hungry cunt. Fill you up nice and full with my cum. Since you came in begging for it tonight."

"I didn't beg for—"

I pull her hair back and start fucking her, not too fast at first. "Don't tell me you aren't desperate for it. You want it so much, you're making me milk my own prostate to try for more. Isn't that right, nasty girl?"

I doubt that's why, but it's nice to accuse her, nonetheless. I take the goopy lotion I left in a pool on my leg and slather it on my tail and rear entrance.

"No. Wait, you're what? I—"

"You'll get what you want. Here we go." I relax my breathing, pause my movements, and try not to laugh as Tabitha perks up suddenly, watching me.

The thin tip of my tail slides in easily. My muscle stretches around the lightly textured limb easier than I expected due to the gradual taper. By the time it gets to its full girth, I'm stretched decently wide, groaning, sweat coating my brow, but from the intensity and pleasure, not pain. My tail—having a mind of its own as usual—refuses to stop wiggling even though it's inside of me. The feeling is…well, it's alien, for sure, but not bad. *Definitely* not bad. I can't help but begin to thrust into Tabitha again, this time faster and harder than before.

"Oh fuck," I repeat mindlessly under my breath as my tail wriggles and throbs inside me, and Tabitha's cunt squeezes me as I fuck her.

All my plans to talk filthy to her go out the window as my brain goes blank of anything but the pleasure I'm feeling. At one point, I hear Tabitha yell that she's coming. Other than that, I'm a goner until the moment I spurt thick streams of cum into her cunt. Then, I'm falling onto my back, still coming extra spurts as my tail insists on reminding me that it's prehensile. When it all finally ends, and I'm lying there out of breath, with Tabitha kneeling over me, I let my tail finally slide out.

Tabitha looks around at all the mess with raised brows before turning back to me.

"See, I knew you would like it. I'm always right." She sniffs the air. "Why does it smell like mango in here?"

Chapter Seventeen

Tabitha

"It really sucks that you have to be in disguise all the time," Henry says as he watches me wrap another scarf around my neck.

"It's not just for disguise, it's for safety. There's a big crowd today, and I don't want to hurt anyone."

I put my regular layers on at home, but I'm adding a few extras in the car on our way to watch Honor Man's wedding. Even though we'll be watching from the roof, we'll have to go through a crowd to get there.

"Still. It sucks. Someday we'll move away from all of this so you can walk around outside naked if you want."

"I would *not* want to be naked outside, even if I were on my own private island. Anyway, you would have to convince the bureau that I'm not a threat before I could leave the city. Good luck with that."

We park a few blocks away from Waljean's and cut through the least busy areas we can. The view of Capital Square is poor from down here, and parking is slim, so there aren't too many people. We managed to get to the store and up to the roof without any issues. Our view of the area where the ceremony is to take place is excellent. There are massive screens above the square that will broadcast it so that we'll actually see their faces. There are a *ton* of people in the crowd below, but I suppose people will want to celebrate with the man who saved so many of them.

Henry and I sit on top of a piece of scrap that was left up here and wait, just talking about life. It's a rare time to do nothing, and I enjoy it.

Finally, loud music plays, and on the screen, words pop up.

WE WELCOME YOU TO THE WEDDING OF RONALD JEMISON AND CRISTINA FLORES

The wedding procession begins. I don't recognize the people, except for Sir Cada and Captain Whiz on Honor Man—*Ronald Jemison's*—side. The younger man there must be his son. On the bride's side is a goat Mashie, that I think is his son's wife. A Superhero's son marrying a Mashie was gossip so hot that even I heard about it in prison.

The bride comes down the aisle, escorted by a very proud-looking man. She's adorable, and not at all what I expected; the upper end of middle age, short, full-figured, graying hair, and the sweetest smile I've ever seen. Ronald brightens up like the sun when he sees her. I can't help but glance at Henry because I know that look. When I look at him now, and see him looking at me, it's right there.

Fuck, he really is in love with me.

My chest tightens up as I think of what life would be like without him. Could I go back to how it was before? This brief time I've spent with him, knowing how it is to be treated like a real person, to be treated with respect and kindness, and...well, love, has changed me. No, I can't go back. I don't *want* to go back.

I love him!

Henry starts to turn away to watch the ceremony. I catch his face in my gloved hands and hold his gaze to mine.

"Henry. Don't ever leave me," I say softly. "I need you."

He takes my wrists, eyes searching mine. "Of course. Are you okay?"

"Fantastic. I love you."

Henry inhales in surprise, eyes wide, before he grabs me by the back of the head, presses his mouth to mine, and kisses me hard. The kiss is fast, passionate, desperate, but it says everything it needs to before we break apart.

"I love you so much," he says on exhale.

We smile at each other, fingers tangled together, as the couple on the ground speak their vows. Things are perfect for a few golden moments in the sun on top of Capital City.

And then Henry reaches for his neck, his eyelids flutter, and confusion takes over his features. He pulls out a thin, needle-like object. We both stare at it for a moment before recognition hits me.

"Run." I grab his hand, desperate, but already knowing it's too late.

Henry tries to stand, but his knees buckle underneath him. He slurs out one thing before he can no longer speak.

"Tabitha?"

The tears fall fast, streaming down my cheeks as I try to drag him to the roof exit. I scream in frustration as his limp body refuses to cooperate. When I'm finally near the door, agents from The Bureau for the Management and Study of Aberrant Genetics burst through it. I lunge toward the one going for Henry, but he shoots me with something that knocks me backward, followed by a sting in my neck. The drowsiness hits me even as I'm still too winded to stand. I can only watch as they take the man I love away to who knows where. Before my mouth no longer cooperates, I manage one scream, and watch as they drag him out the door. I lay on the dirty concrete, unable to act as his pink tail disappears from sight.

My eyes shut, and everything goes black.

I wake up hours later in the dark and cold, still on the roof. My head swims in confusion, knowing something is wrong. It takes me only a moment to remember what that something is, and I'm instantly on my feet, sprinting home, running faster than I have in a decade. With shaking fingers, I dig out my phone and dial the first person I think of.

"Tabitha? What's up?" Mark answers, sounding surprised to hear from me.

"They took him. He's gone. The bureau. We have to help him."

"Whoa, wait, what? Just a second, let me get out of bed." There's a rustling sound and a feminine voice in the background that I'm almost positive is Angela. "Okay, explain."

"The bureau. They saw Henry touch me, then they took him. I don't know where he is. You have to help him." I can't help it, but I start crying again.

"What the fuck, Tabitha? You mean *The Bureau* as in the one for powered people? The notoriously secretive and fucked up one?" Something crashes on his end. "I fucking *told* you two to be careful. *Fuck!*"

"I know. I'm sorry."

In the background, I can hear Angela asking what's going on. Mark must cover the phone or something because it's quiet when he tells her to wait just a moment. Then he comes back to me.

"I'll try to get to them through legal channels, but damn it, Tabitha, I don't know. They're.... *fuck.*"

"I'm gonna do everything I can to get him back, I promise." I dodge a group of kids and wipe away my tears. "I don't have to go through the same *channels* you do."

There's silence on his end for a moment before he speaks again. "As your lawyer, I'm going to pretend I didn't hear that."

"Understood."

"Just...find him. Okay?"

"I'll do anything for him, Mark." I think of the look on his face as we sat on the roof, the one he had when I finally realized I loved him. "Anything."

When I hang up, I think of who to call next. I'm about to dial, but her call comes in first. *Klaire.*

"Hey there. Sorry, I'm late. You know how it is," she sighs.

"More past, less future," I repeat for the hundredth time. People always complain that she won't tell them their future, but she rarely gets premonitions. "What's going on? Can you help me?"

"I think so. Something told me to call you and tell you that you need to contact Diamond Washington."

"What? Why? I've never even spoken to her."

She's a *retired* Hero. One who I'm sure has zero interest in speaking to me.

"That's all I know. That if you want help, you should talk to her."

"Thanks, Klaire. I'll see what happens."

"Good luck, Tabby."

How the hell am I supposed to get in contact with her? As soon as I slam the door to my apartment closed, I collapse, sweaty and out of breath, onto my futon and get online. I look up Diamond's home address, but I don't see one. No social media. She has a website with nothing but an old photo and an email address, but who knows how long it will take her to reply—if she even responds to it at all. I decide to send a message anyway while I look for other ways to contact her, since that's all I have.

Ms. Washington,

What you've heard about me probably isn't great. Frankly, my poor reputation was earned. Now, I'm trying my best to be a good person, and I've met someone who's been helping me.

His name is Henry, and he's the only person who can touch me without dying. The agents at The Bureau found that out, then took him somewhere. I don't know what they're going to do to him, but we both know it's not good.

My friend says you might be able to help him. If that's true, will you? Please? He really is a great guy.

Thank you.

Tabitha Lima.

Well, that's that. I spend the next hour researching everything I can about her, but it looks like after she retired, she did what she could to disappear from public life. There's a serious lack of information about her online, despite her long career. It doesn't make sense.

I know they were brought in for questioning about something recently; could that be affecting the lack of search results? I don't know. Even the Bureau doesn't have the power to erase this much about public figures.

Since her son is still in the military, I suppose I could find her through him, but I'd have to get through a lot of very well-armed people to do so. Not exactly sure I'm up to the task. I'll do what I have to, though. Whatever it takes. I'm researching the entrances to Fort Jeffries, in fact, when my phone vibrates with a new email alert.

My hands shake when I see who it's from: Diamond Washington. I open the message and quickly read the short reply.

Miss Lima,

Turn on your television.

-D. Washington

Huh? I switch on my TV, but all that's on is an old episode of My Husband the Hog. I watch the human-Mashie sitcom for a minute, confused, before thinking about sending an email back to ask if there has been a mistake. But then the screen goes black, then bright white, and then the glitching face of a beautiful woman fills the screen.

Though she appears to be a beautiful Black woman in her mid-twenties, I know she's actually in her late eighties. Diamond Washington doesn't age—that's only one of her many powers. She was born naturally gifted, too. Or, mostly. The Capital City government got a hold of her when she was young, like me, and did things to her to...*enhance* her abilities. I think we have some unfortunate things in common.

"Hello, Tabitha," she says. Her voice is staticky but clear.

"Uh, hi. How are you doing that?" I ask.

"I control electricity and sound, and I've been honing my skills for decades. This isn't hard for me, sweetheart," she laughs. "Anyway, we need privacy to discuss this, and email won't cut it."

"Oh, okay." I awkwardly dust the screen with the edge of my sleeve, then sit back. "Discuss away."

"Well, I'm sure you can guess they've taken him to Geiger Falls."

My stomach sinks. Not there. Please.

"I know both you and I have history there," she continues, her voice taking on a darkness I feel connected to. "Personally, I'd like to see the place burn. They shouldn't touch another person ever again."

A surprised laugh escapes me. "I didn't realize you weren't on the side of The Bureau."

"Fuck The Bureau. I was only ever a Hero to help the people, never to help the government. When the whole thing became public with Darkiss, and they made us into their public symbols of patriotism, I told them to kiss my ass."

"I think I love you," I laugh.

"Don't get me wrong, honey, I'm no Villain either. What Darkiss did was wrong. A lot of what you girls did was too. But I know how you got there. I know too damn well how many roads lead to Geiger Falls."

I look at my hand, and shame, fear, and anger fill me all at once. The helplessness of my situation is clear. Then, Diamond's voice comes through again, soft and comforting.

"We're not gonna let your good man become a Villain, Tabitha."

The tears I thought had dried up by now flow again. My words are punctuated by sobs as I reply, "I just don't know what to do. Even if I get him out, where do I go?"

"Do you think you're the only one who's ever needed to disappear? Where do you think Bradley is?"

Bradley—*Stonecrash*. He's been missing for years.

"You know where he is?"

"Do I know? Hell, I put him there. Do what I tell you, exactly as I tell you, and we'll get you both a place to stay. It's gonna sound far-fetched, and it's gonna take some faith on your part. You've got to be willing to lose *everything* to save this man of yours. Are you?"

I smile. "Everything."

Chapter Eighteen

Henry

"Let me out of here, you cockroach dicks!" I scream at the little window on the door in this bare room they have me in. "I swear to god I'll bite your face off and shove it up your asshole!"

The guard walking past taps on the glass with his flashlight. "Aren't you tired of shouting yet? Your threats are getting a little unhinged. Maybe take a nap."

Then the prick walks off to do his rounds, same as he's been doing all night. I scream in frustration. They won't tell me anything or let me talk to anyone. I've been in this nearly empty, beige room for hours with no contact except for the occasional useless guard. I fall onto the thin mattress of the tiny bed and let out a shaky breath, trying to stop myself from crying.

The built-in speaker above the door crackles suddenly, just about scaring the shit out of me. I sit up and listen attentively to the droning voice.

"Henry Rivers. You are to remain seated. You will cooperate with the doctor and any other employees of the institute. If we determine you are not cooperating, the visit will be terminated. Positive behavior will be rewarded with future benefits. Any attempt to harm an employee or to leave any room without permission will be dealt with accordingly and will result in total loss of benefits. Please acknowledge you understand."

I *really* do not want to cooperate with anything that these people do, but I also need to speak to someone. So, I guess I don't have a choice.

"Uh, I understand. I guess."

When the lock clicks, I almost stand instinctively before remembering the *stay seated* part. I grip the edges of the bed tightly to keep myself grounded. A sickly pale woman in a white jacket walks in, two guards close behind her. She holds her hands crossed primly in front of her and smiles a toothy shark-like grin at me.

"Hello, Henry Rivers. I'm Doctor Gia Chase. I hear you have a special ability."

"Sure, yeah. Now, can you just take some of my blood to test or something and let me go?"

"Oh, no. You see, here at The Geiger Falls Institute, we work to get the absolute most out of the citizens of Capital City. Since we know you're immune to Tabitha, we must wonder what other wonderful abilities you might have hidden away that might benefit *all* of our great people. It's for the good of everyone. Don't you want to help people, Henry?"

"No, fuck you, I want to go home," I spit out. It might sound selfish, but I know what these fuckers do to people, and none of it is helping anyone. "You're not supposed to take unwilling people. They passed laws that—"

The doctor looks at the smirking guards as she cuts me off. "Did you hear that? They passed *laws*. We'd better stop. Villains will understand that we're not allowed to do research, and so, of course, they'll stop innovating out of fairness. Because of the *laws*."

We look at each other silently for a moment, her smiling, me stewing in anger, before I speak.

"So, what do you want then? What am I supposed to do?"

"Oh, we'll do a few basic tests. Take some samples to start. Once we know what you're made of, then we'll find out what we can do with you."

"What does that mean exactly?"

"It depends on what we find. I'll keep you updated. For tonight, we'll have dinner brought in—it's late, so it's nothing great, sorry. In the morning, we'll get started." She turns to leave but pauses when she's nearly out of the door. "You'll have to excuse the screams coming from next door. Knowing that the lover of the woman who put him here is close by has got my husband all worked up. Has Tabitha told you about him? No, forget it. No need to discuss ancient history. Ten years is a long time."

My stomach sinks as she sighs dramatically, and I realize who exactly she is. *Doctor Chase was the optometrist's name, so...I'm so fucked.*

If I don't get out of here soon, I won't get out of here alive.

She taps the side of the door and clears her throat. "Goodnight, Henry."

And then the door closes. I'm alone for the next half hour, listening to anguished screams coming from the room next to me. A similar message crackles over the speaker before my dinner arrives to let me know to stay seated while the guard brings the tray in. It's just a turkey sandwich and some milk—which I don't trust at all since I'm in a crazy fucking research facility—but I'm hungry, so I eat it anyway. I was right not to trust it, too, because about two minutes after finishing it, I got woozy and passed out.

I wake up to a nurse taking my blood pressure and temperature. I try to move, but realize I'm strapped down. Great.

"Good morning, Henry. We'll have those straps off in a second. Just didn't want you getting upset when you woke up. We have to take your vitals frequently, and it could be scary for you if you woke up unexpectedly," she says in a voice far too cheery for the situation.

She takes the thermometer out of my mouth and smiles, then the cuff off my arm, puts them away, and types on a tablet. After wheeling her cart out the door, she says something I can't hear to a guard, then pokes her head back inside.

"It was nice meeting you. I'm Nurse Raquel. I'll see you again soon!"

A particularly large and grumpy guard yawns as he enters the room. "Don't make trouble. I'm tired. Breakfast is coming soon."

"Fine," I say. Now I'm starting to understand Tabitha's preference for one-word replies.

He undoes my restraints and leaves, closing the door behind him. Time to wait. It's quiet for a while until they bring me toast, eggs, and juice. I don't feel particularly drugged after eating them. The screaming commences again. I'm not sure how much longer I sit there, maybe a few hours, before the speaker crackles another warning message. Doctor Chase (the one who's not currently screaming next door) arrives.

"Good afternoon, Henry. I hope your morning has been pleasant."

"I'm locked up against my will, and I was drugged last night. So, fuck this."

She shrugs. "We'll be going for an exam. It'll be short, don't worry. Dave here is going to get you ready for the trip, then we'll be on our way."

"I want to call my brother."

"Oh, sorry, we really should explain these things upon arrival. You must earn calls through good behavior. So, cooperate with Dave and start to earn that phone call, okay?"

I want to argue, but will that prevent me from getting my call? Will I be able to earn a call at all, or is this a trick? *Fuck.* The big guard from earlier lumbers into the room, dragging a wheelchair behind him. I make a quick decision. When he gets to me, I sit in the chair. They won't kill me today, right? I'm sure they need me for something. This is probably just for blood samples and that kind of thing. It'll be fine.

"Good boy," she says, and it makes me want to puke. Only Tabitha can say that.

The guard wheels me down a series of long hallways. We go down a couple of different elevators. I'm totally lost by the time we get to a room that looks more like a place to perform surgery than one to take samples. When nurses come in dressed in those blue hairnets and shoe covers, I know I'm in trouble.

"Alright. I'll scrub in. Give him a sedative to get him on the table. Not too much, though—we do need him awake," Doctor Chase says before heading to an open door off to the side.

I try to fight when a nurse comes at me with a syringe, but she gets me. Soon, I can't move my arms, legs, or, well, anything. The guard lifts me onto the table, straps me down—even my head is strapped down—then leaves. The nurses wipe my face with something cold, and then the Doctor returns.

"Nurse Megan, please record."

"Yes, Doctor."

I hear tearing, and then my eyelids lift. No, they're taped open. *What the fuck?*

"Today, we have patient Henry Rivers, a known associate of former subject, Tabitha Lima. Our previous subject's main result is poison skin. Henry is the only person with immunity to Tabitha's poison. His immunity is believed to be related to the opossum DNA from his Mashie status; however, that is currently theoretical. We will perform general tests and run a battery of experiments designed to find out why he is immune. Let us begin our first test."

I hear an electric whir. Above me, a light turns on that shines white into my eyes so brightly I can't see anything else. It burns, but the tape prevents me from shutting my eyelids.

"Nurse Julie, his tongue," Doctor Chase says.

Rubber-gloved hands yank around in my mouth, securing my tongue. I'm fairly sure this is so I can't swallow or bite it. This is a bad sign.

"Two fifty-three P.M. Beginning pain threshold testing on patient Henry Rivers. Starting with the eyes. Nurse Megan, lower the Johnsen device."

Pain threshold testing? What? The electric whirring gets louder, the light brighter. Dark spots form inside the brightness, then slowly grow larger. I realize what they are.

Needles. There are fucking clusters of needles approaching my eyes. I scream, though I know it's no use.

This is what Tabitha went through. She couldn't stop it, and she's so much stronger than I'll ever be. Which means I'm fucking doomed.

"Give him a bit more sedative," the doctor says. She sounds positively cheerful.

Chapter Nineteen

Tabitha

THE CITIZENS OF CAPITAL City insist that super-powered people are divided into Heroes and Villains. They sleep soundly when they believe they know who's wrong, who's right, and that a Hero will always keep them safe.

In Capital City, a murderer is *always* a Villain. Our stories, our reasons why, don't matter to the good, average citizens. It's easy for them to know who's right and who's wrong—a killer is a Villain, and a Hero is the one who stops them from doing it again.

But the world isn't that simple.

Just like the heart requires blood, love requires sacrifice. Sometimes, to do the right thing, you must be willing to die—and willing to kill.

You have to be the Villain.

I'm going to keep the man I love safe no matter what it takes. I'll be the Villain they think I am.

I'll be the Poison Princess one last time.

Between the stones, near the ocean's shore, I stand in the shadows cast by The Geiger Falls Institute. I shove down the memories of the last time I was here. Only panic would come with those, and there's no time for my own worries. Everything is about Henry now.

The cool wind and the spray of the ocean water on my bare fingertips feel so foreign that I get momentarily distracted by the sensation. My black cape flutters in the ocean breeze, and I clutch it against me tightly, shielding myself from the cold. I forgot how little this outfit covers. Thankfully, the cape both warms me and helps me hide among the rocks—two of its many purposes.

Bzzt. The sound isn't loud, but because I'm waiting for it, I hear it. The electric lock on the little-used side door of this rocky, ocean-side storage area disengages. If everything is going as planned, then Diamond's ensured that the security camera glitches for a few seconds—just long enough for me to slip inside. I stumble, and I'm pretty sure I almost pull a muscle in my ass cheek, but I make it inside in time. It seems I've gotten out of shape since my Villain days.

Once inside, I stay flat against the left side wall like Diamond told me to. We discussed this plan in excruciating detail, and I memorized all of it. I wait patiently for the next *bzzt,* then scamper over to a room that used to be an office but is used as storage now. I wait behind boxes, watching the shadows of guards walk past the frosted glass window, and resist the urge to jump out and poison them. I'm being restrained and deserve a reward, as far as I'm concerned.

The door lock buzzes again, and I take the cue to run out, down the hall, five doors to the right, and into the next buzzing door. This room isn't storage, just dark. I wait against a desk, watching the guards go past like before, waiting for the buzz. It comes earlier than I expected. I spring up, ready to leave, but am caught off guard when the door handle turns from the other side.

Into the room walks a stranger in a white lab coat—a doctor or researcher, perhaps. Before they even have a chance to turn on the light, I snatch them by the throat, pull them inside, and shut the door. As I drag them behind the desk, I cover their mouth for the brief few seconds they might have a chance to scream.

Their corpse fits neatly underneath. I feel no guilt about my actions. Anyone wearing a white coat at Geiger Falls is not someone worthy of sympathy.

A bit later, there's the real buzz, and I'm on my way. Now's when things will get tricky. I have to move quickly as I'll be taking staircases and moving in hallways and rooms that may have people in them. Diamond will be watching and giving me signals to let me know where to go, but there's always a chance that something unexpected could happen. Shit, something already has.

I open the first stairwell door and run up the stairs as fast as I can. As strong as I am, the burn still starts pretty fast. *Fuck I'm out of shape.* I don't let it slow me down, though. Lung power won't keep me from my true—

Okay, never mind. I slow down after twelve flights of stairs. There wasn't time to train before this. I pause on a landing to catch my breath. The door buzzes angrily at me. I sigh.

"Fuck, I know," I wheeze out, then continue up the stairs.

On floor twenty, I stop again, but this time it's where I'm meant to be. I catch my breath as I crouch low in the shadows out of sight of the camera, waiting for Diamond to glitch it again without security catching on to us. Someone exits the door. I consider poisoning them, but they don't notice me as they pass, just looking at their phone as they descend the stairs. Lucky them.

Bzzt, then I begin the dance again, going room to room back and forth until I get to one that makes my heart race faster than the run up the staircase did. I'm terrified of what I'm about to do. Diamond didn't explain this part exactly—a lot of this plan is blind faith on my part—but I know it's the most dangerous part of this rescue. It's also the most necessary. I take long, soothing breaths while I wait for my signal, and remind myself that no matter what I have to do, Henry is worth it. And then, *Bzzt.*

I slink quietly out the door, keeping low. There are a lot of people here, but they're on a shift change, chatting with one another. Besides, they would never think that anyone would sneak into *this* area. Why would anyone risk it?

How could anyone be so stupid as to risk waking *Darkiss*?

So, of course, no one is looking when I open his door just enough to slip inside and close it behind me—the girl who's not *stupid*, but *angry* enough to take the risk, as small as it may be.

Then, there he is.

It's strange to see him lying there. They've shaved off all his beautiful black hair. His perfect, porcelain skin, with the perpetual five o'clock shadow, now just looks pale and unshaven. His large, strong frame has lost much of its muscle. Strangely, his eyes are open. They haven't lost the deep, clear blue that was so easy to sink into.

"Are you there?" I whisper. I know he's not, or at least he can't respond, but I can't help saying something. "It's Tabitha. I don't know if you'll feel this or what, but I'm trying to break someone out of here, and I need your help. You know about that, right? Getting people out of here? So, yeah, that's it. I don't know what I'm doing, by the way. Blame Silent Shock if something goes wrong."

I take the paper off the back of the electrodes connected to the device Diamond gave me, stick them to Darkiss's forehead, then connect a wire to some kind of metal headband that's already around his head. Then, I slap another electrode coming from the device onto his chest and connect another cord to his heart monitor. I tuck the device next to him, step back, and look at the mess of wires. It looks fine, I think. I have no idea what any of this is, or does, or what this will do to him, only that it will help Henry somehow. I'm trusting Diamond because I don't have much of a choice otherwise, and because I like her, if I'm to be perfectly honest. Also, I don't know, I think there's a part of me that wanted to see Darren one last time, maybe a little bit.

I'm about to turn to go into the hiding spot by the door when I pause. "One more thing. Thanks for getting me out of here. But... it was fucked up what you did. I can't ever forgive that. Or for letting people think that the other three and I were okay with it. I don't ever want to associate with you again. It's a fucked-up world, Darren, but *fucking hell,* I'm just happy I'm not still stuck in here. I really hope you get out someday and can stop being angry. *Please* don't fucking do shit like that again though."

Then I crouch in a blind spot and wait for the *Bzzt.* When it comes, I slip out and head for the staircase. I run down to the tenth floor, *bzzt,* then into another dark office, and wait again.

Then, shit goes *nuts.*

Alarms go off. Red lights flash in the hall and even in the room where I'm hiding. Over a speaker, a voice says:

WE HAVE A CODE FIFTY ON FLOOR TWENTY. CODE FIFTY ON FLOOR TWENTY. ALL STAFF ENACT SECURITY MEASURES THREAT LEVEL RED. CODE FIFTY ON FLOOR TWENTY. ENACT THREAT LEVEL RED.

The alarms continue to go off, and the message repeats, as people run through the halls. I hear yelling, but don't make out the words, until someone stops outside this room and says, "How the fuck is he awake?"

Since I'm able to put two and two together, I nearly shit my skimpy costume. *Oh, shit.* He really woke up. I thought Diamond was just going to, I don't know, make his vitals spike, or his brainwaves do weird things, so the doctors would panic. Something like that. Not wake him up for real.

Okay. Maybe I am stupid.

Fuck! I can feel the bile in my stomach rising, and I concentrate on holding it down. There's no time to puke. I wait for the *Bzzt,* and when it comes, I dash out and into the next room.

There I find him, my Henry, sitting on a thin, shitty bed just like the one I used to have.

"Henry! It's me!" I say.

I have to tell him out loud who I am because *his eyes are fucking swollen and bleeding.* What did those monsters do to him?

Wait. Not the pain tests. I look at his hands and see that they're bandaged. He turns stiffly to look at me, and when he smiles, the corners of his lips crack and turn red with fresh blood.

They did it to him. My knees buckle, and I have to catch myself on the handle of the door to keep from falling.

"Tabitha? It's really you?" he says thickly. From experience, I know his tongue must hurt.

"Yes. Don't talk, just heal. I'm getting us out of here. Come here and wait with me. When this door makes a buzzing sound, we run. Stop when I tell you, okay? A friend is helping us."

"You're so fucking cool," he says with a laugh that makes me smile and cry at the same time.

"You're so annoying. You made me cry," I say as I wipe away tears.

He drapes his arm around my shoulder, and I feel the exhaustion weighing heavily on him. He huffs.

"Hey, I got tortured because of you." He takes hold of my hand. "You're not wearing gloves. Did you kill anyone?"

"Yes. Are you mad?"

"Not even a little bit. These people fucking suck."

The door buzzes, and we're off, moving slower now that I have him with me. An idiot guard with a huge gun pops out of a doorway, shouting, and shoots at us. I whirl around, covering us in my bulletproof cape, as I discover something unfortunate. Apparently, that's about all my poor Henry can handle for now.

He told me the only trait he inherited from the opossum was the tail. As I watch Henry's body go still, his breathing slows to almost nothing, and his tongue flops out of his mouth; as his eyes roll back, his heartbeat nearly stops, his hands curl up, and he releases a stench like rotting flesh; I look at the dead weight in my arms and realize Henry was wrong. He inherited one more trait, and now I'll have to fight my way out of this place as he plays dead.

This *love* thing is much harder than I initially assumed.

"Stay here," I whisper as I drop my stiff, stinking lump of a boyfriend behind a pillar.

I wrap my cape around me, and when a light in front of the trigger-happy guard suddenly flashes right in his eyes, I rush forward. All it takes is one slap to his stupid face, and he's down. I form a heart with my hands as a thanks to Diamond for the help with the flashing light, then slide back to Henry.

"Okay. Let's go, Stinky."

I put him under my cape and over my shoulder, then away we go. The halls are empty now that the staff is hiding or evacuated, so we go all the way to the stairs without stopping. More stairs. Now with added weight. Fuck my life.

Down the annoying steps I go, determined to move to a place that only has one floor once I'm out of here. At the shadowy blind spot, the door buzzes to let me know to keep going. A few floors down, it buzzes again, but on this floor, I'm not sure if it's telling me to pause or to move on. As I'm trying to remember, someone in a white coat comes through the door. Someone I recognize.

Doctor Chase.

Well, not the Doctor Chase I knew up close and personal. This one I only know from photos and her courtroom appearance.

"Oh, hello, Tabitha. Hello, Henry," she says. "How nice to see the lovely couple reunited. I wasn't aware it was visiting hours."

I carefully set Henry against the wall, then flex my hands. Doctor Chase holds her tablet in front of her, looking unafraid. Two huge guards come through the door and loom menacingly behind her.

"Hi, how's hubby?" I ask. "He still doing the whole hallucinating and writhing in pain thing, or has he decided to try something new?"

Her smile falters for only a split second before she responds. "Oh, he's improving. He has a room right next to your sweetheart. I made sure to visit them both, one right after the other."

"I'm sure you had a lovely visit after you did the pain tests on Henry, didn't you?"

"Very lovely," she says, her smile widening. "Though, I must say, Henry's pain threshold isn't very high. He's going to have to learn to take more if he's going to survive our research. You remember how things are, right, Tabitha?"

"I remember. I made sure your husband knows what it felt like. You know, I wonder what other sorts of demons his mind has conjured up. Do you ever wonder about that? He was so creative with his torture. I bet he comes up with some wild stuff in there. Judging by his screams, it really seems like—"

"That's enough, you freak whore," she snaps.

It's my turn to smile. *Got her.*

"That's not very professional."

"You're lusting over a half-breed, Tabitha. Look at him! It's pathetic. You should be grateful you're part of something bigger. This place made you special. Without my husband, you'd be gutter trash," she snarls.

I feel a growl in my chest. I don't care what people say to me, but him? No one talks about him like that.

"I'm done here, Doctor Chase. Henry and I are leaving." I flex my neck, knowing full well this isn't going to go that easily.

"Fine then." She gestures to the guards behind her. "Put the animals down."

Sigh. Yep, nothing can ever be easy. I brace myself as they lurch forward. The men are covered in heavy material from head to toe. They've clearly prepared for touch-specific abilities, but that's not a problem for me. I may be out of shape, but there's one thing I've kept strong—and that's my mind.

Darkiss trained me to always keep track of even the tiniest of exposed places, or places where coverage could be easily removed. The other girls and I knew we were at a disadvantage to many superheroes, because we needed skin-to-skin contact to use our abilities. If they could just cover up, we had to get good at finding and creating weak spots.

Then, there's the gear. We refer to our outfits as *costumes,* but there's much more to them than looks. The flexibility of my minimal, stretchy clothing is what allows me to crouch low when the guard reaches out to grab me, and to kick his leg out from under him. I flip my cape—already proven its usefulness several times today—over his head, and wrap it around him. Now that the guard is blinded and unable to move, I pull a thin dagger from the side of my boot, pierce the soft, weak point in his armor, and tear a hole big enough for my fingers.

I've practiced this series of moves hundreds of times. Even out of shape and years out of practice, it's still burned into my muscle memory. It only takes seconds until my hand is inside his shirt.

The second guard, who'd already begun to hesitate when he saw how quickly I moved, steps backward toward the exit door. As his comrade's shrieks fade to silence, I lock eyes with him and kindly offer him a choice.

"You can leave, or you can die. Either way is fine with me."

He chooses the exit.

"Well, he won't be employed here much longer," Doctor Chase grumbles. "Really can't find good help these days."

I kick the lifeless body of the first guard down the stairs and plant my feet. Henry... drools.

"You have a choice too," I say. "Die or live, screaming, like your husband."

"Thank you for the offer, Miss Lima, but I think I'll be going."

She darts toward the exit, moving faster than I would have expected. Before she gets there, however, she trips, falling face-first to the floor with a *crack*. I look down at her and laugh. Henry's tail is wrapped around her ankle. Even when the rest of him is out of commission, his tail, apparently, still does whatever it wants.

"I don't think you will," I say. "So, I'll decide for you."

I crouch low, pinch the leg of her pants, and pull it up just enough to reveal a sliver of skin. She screams and begs for mercy. None of that matters to me. If I had the chance to punish her a thousand times, I'd still take one more.

She tried to kill me.

She hurt my Henry.

"Say hi to the other Doctor Chase—if you're ever able to speak coherently, that is."

With that, I barely graze her skin with the tip of my pinkie, sit back on my heels, and wait. Her screams of fear turn into shrieks of agony and terror. Madness dances in the corners of her eyes, waiting for its chance to take over completely. Good.

"Alright, Henry. We can go now." I chuck him over my shoulder again and continue our descent.

We exit into dark, overcast skies, and grey waves splashing loudly onto the shore. Scientists are fleeing the building, and the military is arriving. I stumble along the uneven rocks and sand—not the ideal terrain for carrying a man who's playing possum. Thankfully, I soon spot the large cluster of stones by the shore that I'm looking for.

When we get closer, I can make out a small boat hiding between them. In these waves, we're going to have a bitch of a time paddling out, but Diamond says we don't have to get far. That's all I know. Get in this boat and row until someone gets us to our next spot. She said she couldn't risk telling me anything else. I'm risking everything, knowing nothing, except that I'm doing it for Henry. That's all that matters.

I drag his heavy, lovable butt into the boat, then paddle us out to sea. I'm worried we'll be spotted, but with all the commotion over Darkiss, they're not watching this side of the island very carefully.

Though the fear makes it feel like ages, we're not out long before I see a bigger boat. There's no way to be certain it's the one I'm looking for, but the little lightning bolt on the side makes me think this is the right one.

"Almost there, Henry," I say as I row to the side of it.

They haul us up, careful not to touch me, and a little confused about Henry. Once onboard, I kneel on the deck for several minutes, not hearing what anyone is saying, just trying not to cry. Breathing the air. Grateful to be away from Capital City. Mostly, though, I still can't believe someone, a whole boatful of people, was willing to help us. It's so much to take in at once, and I need to absorb it before I can move on.

But then Henry's arms are around me, and my head is on his shoulder, and the world makes sense. I don't have to be a Villain. I'm just Tabitha, a girl on a boat, with her super sweet boyfriend.

"Hey, you gotta get up. These people need to talk to us. Okay?" he says quietly and kisses me on top of my head.

I nod and reach out to touch him, making sure he's alright now. He smiles.

"There's a healing lady here. Pretty cool. She woke me up. Sorry, I stink."

"I'll have to thank her. And, uh, no worries. I'll take a living boyfriend that smells like garbage over a dead one any day." I rub his belly, trying to hold in a laugh. "I wonder if you'll grow a pouch now. Anything's opossumble."

"Glad you prefer me alive. Not glad that you're making bad puns. Now, come on. Say hi." He stands and offers his hand to me, which I gladly take.

The few people who are on the boat—aside from the captain, who is currently sailing as fast as he can away from Geiger Falls—are waiting for us inside the cabin. They stand nervously on the far side, but they all wave hello, and no one is rude. A woman, who looks a little familiar, steps forward and introduces herself.

"Hello. I'm Amelia. Diamond is my mother."

Ah, so that's why she looks familiar. Diamond kept her and all of this a secret. I've been desperate to ask questions. Now's my chance.

"Hi, Amelia. I'm—well, you know who we are. Thank you for saving us. Diamond says other people have been saved before. How is it you all haven't been caught?"

"Well, that's my whole thing—not being seen when I don't want to be. The folks in Capital City don't even know I exist."

Henry looks at me, then back at her. "How is that possible? If you're Diamond's kid, then they must have a record of you."

"She had me *before* they found her. When she was a kid herself, sadly, she got pregnant and was kicked out of her home. Moved in with an aunt way out on a farm. Birthed me right there, no hospital record. When they came and took her away, I was still little. She told me to hide, not to ever let them find me. That's when I discovered I could be invisible. Not just to the eye but to the mind. My aunt and I worked on enhancing my abilities, secretly. I learned to use it on other people, and eventually on entire cities." She squeezes the hand of the woman next to her. "So that's how we get away.

Where we're going, they won't find us, because they don't even know to look."

**

We sail for hours before making it to land. I'm nervous but excited to leave the ship. Will people accept me here? Or did I leave one place that hates me, just to get to another? The smiling face I see when I step off the boat is a good sign.

"Bradley?"

The scarred man runs forward, stopping close enough for me to see the broken tooth in the center of his silly grin.

"Hey, Tabby," he says. "Welcome home."

Henry wraps his tail around my waist as we head to the registration office to be assigned a place to live. All the places we pass look clean and well-kept. No dilapidated, roach-filled Villain housing.

"Is this real?" I ask Henry, laughing, but a little serious too. "They know I'm a Villain, right?"

"Tabitha, I don't think that matters here."

When we get to the registration office, they ask us about our skills, our limitations, that sort of thing. They give us a starter place to stay—a tiny cabin—a stipend for food, and other basics. The worker there says we'll get some time to relax and get to know people in the town.

We'll get set up with a therapist, she says, so we can learn to adjust to our new way of life. According to her, new people sometimes have a tough time learning not to be anxious, greedy, suspicious, or violent, because they've always had to be that way out of necessity or force. That therapy is necessary for most people.

She says they'll take our skills, limitations, abilities, and preferences into consideration and apply them to what's needed around the island. We'll get jobs when we're settled in.

I tell her I don't trust it. That every time I've seen something this good in a movie, it ends up being a weird death cult or something. She tells me that's a normal reaction, and assures me that this isn't a utopia, and she's making no claim that it is. It only seems perfect because the place we come from treated us so poorly. She says once we get going, we'll be complaining about work, chores, and back aches as we would anywhere else. That being treated with fairness and kindness will soon seem like the normal thing it always should have been.

When we leave for our new place, Henry and I shower, then lie in bed together quietly until we both fall asleep.

In the morning, everything begins fresh.

Chapter Twenty

Tabitha

"Tabitha, tell me about your mother."

I roll my eyes at Henry and throw a handful of weeds at him. Laughing, he bats it away. It's Sunday, he doesn't have to teach at the school today, and we can enjoy lunch together in our yard, in the grass, in the sun.

"Eat your carrots. I can see you avoiding them."

They import things here, of course, and there are a couple of small farms. Any additional veggies, we grow in our little garden. We ended up with *a lot* of carrots this year, and Henry is obviously getting sick of them. *Too bad.* I worked hard on that garden.

"Eh, I'm not avoiding them. I'm just waiting for the right time."

"Uh-huh. Sure."

He shrugs and stabs a carrot with his fork, sliding it around on his plate. His face turns solemn.

"It was hard to get Jimmy to eat carrots. One of the last times I babysat him was a carrot day, actually."

"I'm sorry, Henry. I know you miss Mark and Jimmy."

"The video was nice. I hope I get another one."

On Henry's birthday, Amelia handed him a package. Inside was a DVD—we all have DVD players as our one source of entertainment tech on the island—and on it was a video of Mark, Angela, and Jimmy. They let him know that they knew he was safe, they missed him, they were okay, they loved him, and that they hoped to see him again soon. They told him about their daily life, and it was so sweet. He cried the whole time through it, and has watched it at least a dozen times since.

"Maybe I'll get one on my birthday." I smile. "Don't worry, though, Henry. I know we'll see them again someday. I have a feeling."

"Thanks, Tabitha." He slides the carrot around some more, possibly trying to fool me into thinking he's eating it. He sighs. "You could make me feel better now by telling me about your mother."

I shove his knee. "Why do you care?"

"I'm serious, I want to know more about your history. Stuff before your whole Villain arc." He hands me the daisy he plucks from beside our garden. "Have a flower."

I don't tell him that it's the only flower I've ever been given, but I do tuck it behind my ear. His face lights up.

"Okay, that looks amazing," he says. "Absolutely gorgeous. Nature goddess right there."

I wave at him dismissively, so he'll stop before I start blushing too hard. Then, I sigh in resignation. I knew I'd have to tell him about her eventually.

"Fine. I'll tell you about my mom, since apparently, we've gotten so bored here, we have nothing better to do than yap and yap all day."

I smooth out my long, black skirt while Henry gets in a comfortable position, and then begin.

"My dad was a creep who pretended to love her. He promised her all sorts of things, as long as she left her country and moved to Capital City with him when she turned eighteen. She did. They got married, and she got pregnant. He left her alone in the city with nothing and no one. Luckily, she was smart, resilient, and kind, so she made friends quickly and found good work. I know those things from talking to a former neighbor. If you asked me what I knew about my family history aside from that, I couldn't tell you anything."

Henry rubs my hand as I speak, and I use his loving energy to help me go on.

"I don't remember a lot about her, because I was only three when she died, and when she was alive, she was gone at work most of the day. I don't even remember what she looked like, Henry, which hurts a lot. I do remember that she smelled good, and that she had a beautiful smile, and that I was so happy when she held me. I remember when she died. She got hit by a car. Gone, just like that."

Henry attempts to hug me, but I stop him. I'm not done.

"I was scared when they took her body away, and I ran off. I didn't want them to put me in a bag, too; that was all I could think. I hid for days, and when someone found me, I refused to tell them who I was. It took them so long to figure it out that I missed my mom's funeral. When they told me I'd never see her again, I lost my shit. Tore the place up and threw my tiny fists at the social workers. So then they labeled me a troublemaker. Threw me into a foster home that—"

I brush that memory back into the dark corner where it needs to stay.

"Well, one day, I ran away from that place. When they found me, they put me into a second, worse situation. Little me didn't think that was possible. That's how I found out anything's possible if someone's fucking evil enough. My life went on like that, one shitty thing after the other." I wipe a tear off my cheek. "Fuck, Henry. I was just a little girl who wanted her mom, but I found monsters every time."

When he reaches for me, this time I let Henry hold me.

"That little girl never had a chance, Henry. It's not fair. The moment I was born, I was destined to fail. I was always going to end up a Villain."

He buries his face in my hair, breathes in deeply. On the exhale, he pulls away just enough to speak quietly, his forehead to mine.

"It's true that you were set on that path. I can't deny that. The number of people who hurt you when you were so innocent is horrifying. Whether you take vengeance on them makes you a Villain, I suppose, is debatable. But the people who hurt you will never get a shred of sympathy from me. You took all that pain, all the horror, and you still wake up every day, trying to be good. Not everyone could do that. There are so many people who love you now, too. You may have had a few bad years, but to me, you will never be a Villain."

"A few bad years, huh?"

"Just a few."

"I love you so much. You've always made me feel like a real person again." I pull away, smooth out his unruly hair, and look him in the eyes. "Hey, do you think they do weddings here? We could get married."

He's silent for a moment, blinking several times before replying.

"Are you asking me to marry you?"

"Yeah."

"One-word responses again? At a time like this?" His fork clatters to his plate. "Where are the beautiful poems and romantic speeches to swoop me off my feet? Can I get one of those?"

"No."

Henry laughs and tackles me to the grass. "Alright, fine. I'll take you as you are, you grumpy goddess. I love you. Always."

Always.

"We'll be safe here, right, Henry?"

A cloud passes over us. It could feel ominous, but my Henry doesn't let it. He smiles and smooths my hair back. "Don't worry, Tabitha. I'll protect you."

I smile back and tell him that I believe him.

I look him dead in the eye, serious as a funeral, and press my lips to his ear.

"Go eat your carrots."

Thank You

I WANT TO SAY a special thank you to my alpha and beta readers. I read every comment and each one meant so much. Michaela, Ellie, Alijay, Ginger, Max, Latrexa, and May: you rock!

Goat Girl

Can I believe in heroes when the world treats me like a villain?